INHERITANCE OF CRISES AND DYSFUNCTION

JAMES J. MAIWURM

iUniverse

INHERITANCE OF CRISES AND DYSFUNCTION

Copyright © 2020 James J. Maiwurm.

All rights reserved. No part of this book may be used or reproduced by any means, graphic, electronic, or mechanical, including photocopying, recording, taping or by any information storage retrieval system without the written permission of the author except in the case of brief quotations embodied in critical articles and reviews.

This is a work of fiction. All of the characters, names, incidents, organizations, and dialogue in this novel are either the products of the author's imagination or are used fictitiously.

iUniverse books may be ordered through booksellers or by contacting:

iUniverse
1663 Liberty Drive
Bloomington, IN 47403
www.iuniverse.com
844-349-9409

Because of the dynamic nature of the Internet, any web addresses or links contained in this book may have changed since publication and may no longer be valid. The views expressed in this work are solely those of the author and do not necessarily reflect the views of the publisher, and the publisher hereby disclaims any responsibility for them.

Any people depicted in stock imagery provided by Getty Images are models, and such images are being used for illustrative purposes only. Certain stock imagery © Getty Images.

ISBN: 978-1-6632-0466-0 (sc)
ISBN: 978-1-6632-0468-4 (hc)
ISBN: 978-1-6632-0467-7 (e)

Library of Congress Control Number: 2020913224

Print information available on the last page.

iUniverse rev. date: 07/27/2020

CONTENTS

Acknowledgments vii

Chapter 1   Back Home? 1
Chapter 2   Inaugural Reactions 7
Chapter 3   Back to Georgie's 10
Chapter 4   Life amid the Moving Boxes 21
Chapter 5   Cutting Ties to the Past 25
Chapter 6   Getting to Know Margie 27
Chapter 7   Beltway Beckons 31
Chapter 8   Enter Louise 34
Chapter 9   Selling Salt at the White House 37
Chapter 10 Small Town America Issues I 42
Chapter 11 Farming in the New Normal 48
Chapter 12 Louise and Salt Talk Turkey 53
Chapter 13 Canadian Reality Check 58
Chapter 14 Napkin Principles 66
Chapter 15 Napkin Negotiations 72
Chapter 16 White House Input 75
Chapter 17 Global Briefing 101 80
Chapter 18 Small Town America Issues II 84
Chapter 19 Small Town America Issues III 87
Chapter 20 Food for Thought; Small Town America Issues IV 92
Chapter 21 London 99
Chapter 22 London: Further Reflections 106
Chapter 23 London: More Serious Chats 112
Chapter 24 Off Ramp: Middle Eastern Diversion 119
Chapter 25 Iranian Backgrounder I; Tracks in the Snow 123
Chapter 26 Walk in the Park, Talk, and More 127
Chapter 27 Berlin Bearings 132
Chapter 28 Iranian Backgrounder II 135

Chapter 29 German Minister Cameo 139
Chapter 30 Berlin: Next Steps 142
Chapter 31 Berlin: Game Plan Emerges 146
Chapter 32 Berlin: Straight Talk 148
Chapter 33 On to Prague 151
Chapter 34 Facing the Iranian Front 155
Chapter 35 Back on the Farm 162
Chapter 36 Georgie's: Progress toward the Middle 165
Chapter 37 Suits Salt 169
Chapter 38 Rough Seas in DC 173
Chapter 39 Confession: Good for the Soul and the Mission 176

ACKNOWLEDGMENTS

As stated elsewhere, this is a work of fiction. The book does not rely on substantive input from others. It is based in large part on personal perceptions of the news of the day and imagination as to the future. However, given the subject matter of this novel, it would be wrong not to take advantage of an opportunity to express the thanks that all of us owe to groups of dedicated, able, patriotic, and, yes, brave Americans whose service motivates this book.

These include members of the US diplomatic corps and intelligence community for all they do—and do very well. Prominent examples include Marie L. Yovanovitch and Lt. Col. Alexander Vindman (Ret.), to whom we all owe not only thanks for their service but also an apology for their treatment in early 2020. How we got to the need to communicate both thanks and an apology in the same sentence is anomalous. But it is an example of what motivates this book.

They also include health care workers everywhere who answered the call to assist in caring for the multitudes affected by the COVID-19 virus while facing the risk of enhanced personal exposure. How extraordinarily brave and essential are these frontliners.

And thanks as well to the hundreds of thousands of diverse and non-violent protesters who are reminding—or perhaps teaching—us that black lives matter, in the broadest sense of that phrase.

All of these are the kinds of people who will help us cope with our inheritance of crises and dysfunction. We need them, and more like them.

CHAPTER ONE

Back Home?

Inauguration Day, January 2021. Gray. Damp. Chilly.

For Staunton Pepper, the only thing not depressing about the day was that President Anthony Pope was about to leave office. After a close, divisive, and uninspiring but somewhat frightening election, President Evans had emerged. Evans presented as progressive enough to attract a sufficient number of millennials and minority voters but not so progressive as to alienate most moderates and suburbanites. He accepted and promoted the need for different approaches to the COVID-19 pandemic and the related recession that remained scourges, won the popular vote, and managed not to lose in places where the electoral college could have—once again—overcome the popular voting results. From Pepper's standpoint, things could have turned out much worse, but it was unclear how much improvement had actually been achieved. Only time and actual actions and reactions would tell. The good news was it wasn't his problem.

Pepper turned on the only radio he could find, an AM clock radio, complete with static, in time to listen to President Evans's inaugural address in the early afternoon. The speech was better than the last one—President Pope's—but not very detailed or, until the end, inspiring. In concluding his speech, President Evans said:

> Fellow citizens of the United States and the world, we are burdened with an inheritance of crises and dysfunction that does not respect political or national boundaries. But we are blessed with the means and ability to respond. We will succeed if, instead of being distracted by trying to assess blame, we recognize that we are indeed in this together. Our mandate is to overcome the tyranny of our inheritance and chart a better course for all. We can and we will. That starts today.

Pepper thought the speech was a little like an Olympic balance beam program that was pretty good overall but punctuated by the sticking of a very high and flawless landing for a ten.

Pepper had his own crises on his hands. At least they seemed like crises to him. He had just moved from a three-bedroom condominium in the District of Columbia to his family farm in central Virginia on the eastern edge of the Blue Ridge Mountains. He had been gone for more than forty years. The movers left after finishing their new practice of applying a fog of disinfectant on everything they had moved. Pepper was alone and surrounded by a sea of boxes—all sizes and shapes—and he had not a clue about how and where to begin dealing with the mess.

Pepper was a lawyer by training, not very handy, lacking practical organizational skills, and still adjusting to his wife's death seven months earlier, in June 2020, during the initial stages of the COVID-19 crisis. He had even moved some of her things—some without knowing it. To make things worse, he wasn't a label person. Neither were his discount movers. As he considered his fate, he pulled a large box off the couch in what seemed to be his living room so there was a place to sit down. Just for grins, he tried to figure out where the contents of that box might go. It was heavy and large, but he had no hint of what its contents were. It seemed to him that anyone coming by to visit would conclude that he was hopelessly clueless. Why would someone without practical farming experience, and a recent widower without friends in the area to boot, move to the middle of nowhere near the edge of the Blue Ridge Mountains during January?

As he sat down and put his legs up on another box, Pepper pondered what the hell he had been thinking when he decided to move. He sat there motionless and glum for a bit. And then things got worse: he heard a sound that could only be the doorbell.

Sure enough, it was. A woman carrying a small box of something had appeared uninvited on his porch. He was still thinking through what it meant to have something you might call a porch; he had not lived anywhere with something like that since leaving the farm to go to college in the Midwest. As he looked out the window of the door, he noticed that it had started to rain and observed that a porch protected uninvited visitors from the elements. Which way did that cut?

Panicked, Pepper looked down to remind himself of what he had on. Sweatpants, an old hoodie that he had once worn while painting a room in his old apartment, and ancient tennis shoes that showed their age. He had not yet shaved, and his hair was unkempt at best. In contrast, he could tell that his tallish visitor was wearing a dress under her raincoat and had well-groomed hair and black flat shoes that were not showing signs of age. She also seemed to be wearing a smile under her mask.

Pepper broke through his introverted nature, summoned all of his courage, and opened the door. He concluded by her cheerful "Welcome to the neighborhood" that they were not going to get along.

She introduced herself as Margaret Hatcher. "Not Thatcher," she said. "Call me Margie. Everyone does. I live down the road about half a mile and noticed the moving truck pulling away. I was baking some chocolate chip cookies today and thought you might be able to use a sugary energy booster."

Pepper was standing in the doorway holding the door half-closed when it finally dawned on him that he was being impolite and had no choice but to invite her in. And there was the chocolate chip cookie factor—homemade chocolate chip cookies scored big points.

Pepper stumbled a bit but managed to say, "I'm embarrassed by the state of things here, but please come in and allow me to find a place where you might safely sit down at a proper social distance, and let me find one of my unused masks. I'm sure I have some somewhere."

"Not to worry," she said. "I'll keep my distance, and there is no such thing as an easy and orderly move. We Welcome Wagon volunteers see all kinds of disasters."

"Welcome Wagon?" queried Pepper. "I didn't know it still existed."

"Well, it actually doesn't—at least not here in a formal way," explained Margie. "But a few of us in a book club try to do what we can to help newcomers adjust to Carterville and feel welcome. It's just the right thing to do, and we meet some very interesting people this way. Will your family be joining you today?"

"Sorry to say I don't have a family," explained Pepper. "My wife passed last year, and we didn't have children. So, other than a younger sister, I'm on my own."

"I am so sorry. I didn't intend to open wounds," she said sincerely.

"Your question was perfectly natural—and no harm done."

"Thanks," said Margie. "If you don't mind another risky question, what brings you here?"

"I shouldn't admit this, but to be honest, I was just sitting here wondering that myself," mused Pepper. "What am I doing here? The obvious answer is that I grew up here, on this farm, until I went off to college. Although I never came back, except for holidays, it ended up being mine when my parents passed. My sister didn't want it, and I was willing to take the farm as my share of the estate. At that time, the Yoder family was actually farming here, and when my parents passed, the Yoders moved into the house. They couldn't afford to buy the farm, and I hated to sell it out from under them, though I'm told that 150 acres is really not big enough to work financially. They were good, hardworking folks who treated it like it was theirs. I never made much on the deal, but I didn't need much."

"I didn't know the Yoders well," said Margie, "but they seemed like nice folks."

"They are," said Pepper. "They decided to retire from farming toward the end of 2019. Jack Davis, who went to school with my sister and is younger than me, called and said he wanted to rent the land and barn to be part of his farming operations, but he wasn't interested in buying. So, as I was winding down with my law firm in DC in the wake of my wife's death and the dislocation created by the COVID-19 virus, it seemed like coming back home might make for a good, fresh start for the rest of my life." He paused, looking out the window toward the mountains but not really focusing on anything, and then commented as much to himself as to Margie, "Holy cow. I'm sorry to burden you with my life history. I've got to watch that."

"That's okay. I asked the question," she replied.

"Okay, Margie. Turnabout is fair play," said Pepper. "What's your story? Are you from around here?"

"Yes and no," she said. "I attended James Madison University, about forty miles south of here. I was dating my husband-to-be at the time, and we were both education majors at Madison. He was from Carterville, and I was from a suburb of Philadelphia. We both student taught here in town and ended up with offers in what was not a great market for teachers. After we graduated, we got married and moved here. He was a teacher and basketball coach. He coached junior high and then freshmen and eventually the boys' varsity basketball team. I taught high school English and ended up as the assistant principal at the high school."

"Any children?" asked Pepper.

"No," she replied. "I guess we were overexposed to kids at school, so we never had our own. He passed away several years ago in an auto accident, but I didn't have it in me to move. Besides, for better or worse, we knew virtually everyone around these parts, and my friends and support infrastructure were all here. In that sense, I'm now from here."

"Sorry," said Pepper. "Now I'm the one who's ripping off scabs."

"Don't worry," she said. "I have some scar tissue but no open wounds. Back to you. Do you need some help here? How are you planning to get unpacked and settled in all by yourself? I would be glad to come over tomorrow in jeans and help out."

"You just put your finger on the problem," he responded. "I don't have a clue about how I'm going to unpack. My current thinking is that I'm going to find and deal with the minimum I need and then put the rest on hold to see how this move works for me. No offense, but it could be that the whole move here is a massive mistake. I don't know, and won't for a while. In any event, thanks, but I think I can handle the bare necessities."

"Okay." She smiled. "I get that. But holler if your new neighbors can help at all. I'm just down the road about half a mile toward town."

"There are a couple of things you could help with," Pepper said. "I could use some recommendations. In no particular order, I need to get a haircut, have some dry cleaning done, and find an informal place to eat that's open for indoor dining and not a fast-food joint."

"Those are easy ones." She laughed. "Dry cleaner is on the edge of town on the left. As for the haircut, do you want a stylist or a barber?"

"A barber."

"Then try Georgie's on the square in town," she said. "You'll either love it or hate it."

"OMG, is this the same Georgie's that was in business when I left home to go to college?"

"The same." Margie smiled. "And there is a good small town diner called Helen's Place across the street from Georgie's near the county courthouse in the middle of town."

"Wow. This will be a serious trip down memory lane."

"Well," responded Margie, "you almost missed them. They are small businesses that were shut down for more than two months last spring as a result of the COVID-19 pandemic. Things remained slow even after the lockdown eased up, and I guess they still are. I'm not sure which of the small businesses will make it over the long term. Things have been rough for a long time."

"These have been tough times indeed," remarked Pepper. "Heaven knows when we'll return to normal, whatever that is."

"Well, good luck with deciding what you're going to do," Margie said as she stood up and headed for the door, "and let me know if there's anything I can help with. My number is on this card."

After Margie left, Pepper returned to his ruminations and box collection. He concluded that the first day in a new place must always be miserable.

CHAPTER TWO

Inaugural Reactions

Many around the United States and the rest of the world paid more attention to the Evans inaugural address than Pepper did. For example, at both Number 10 Downing Street and the home of the Foreign and Commonwealth Office on King Charles Street in London, British officials were huddled around television sets to take in the address and then—after taking off their masks and with inspiration provided by some scotch (rather than the weaker and more common gin and tonic)—assess what the speech meant. At Downing Street, Prime Minister Eleanor Holmes's verdict was short and to the point: "Well, I guess it is better to learn nothing than to be scared to death."

The foreign secretary's team at the Foreign and Commonwealth Office had a more vigorous discussion about the admittedly hidden meaning of the new president's scant reference to foreign policy and returning the United States to a role of collaboration, leadership, and consensus building. They were more positive in their assessment. After thirty minutes of debate and two scotches on the rocks Foreign Secretary John Watson asked, "Just what the hell is Stuart Bacon up to these days?"

Bacon had worked on the Evans campaign, had bona fide qualifications and experience in the US foreign service, and was a favorite to land some outward-looking role in the new administration, but nobody knew what. Many speculated that he would gain the secretary of state's seat at the table; others thought something in the US intelligence community was more likely. The new president had not hinted at anything yet but would have to nominate someone to something soon.

The transition to the new Evans administration had been anything but smooth. First, there was the election itself. The COVID-19 pandemic, which had created some truly exasperating experiences in some of the mid-2020 primary elections, had forced a movement toward new and somewhat experimental voting methods. This made turnout predictions and polling even less reliable than in the past. And of course there were concerns about security of the election results from foreign interference, which some thought had been invited by President Pope, and the risk of voting fraud. The term *rigged* seemed to be on everyone's tongue and in court papers. There was litigation challenging the election results that had made it to the Supreme Court, which finally declared a stop to the circus in the courts and allowed the Evans transition team to begin to get in gear. But a precious six weeks had been lost, and the Pope administration had not been exactly magnanimous in terms of cooperation. In short, the new Evans presidency was still climbing out of a bunker (or perhaps more accurately, a basement). These diversions had prevented the normal level of focus on things diplomatic.

To make matters worse, President Evans was a newcomer to the international scene, having focused on the myriad serious domestic US issues during the campaign. So the experts outside of the United States were largely guessing when spouting opinions of what the new US administration would mean for the somewhat tattered state of US foreign relations.

The British Foreign Service team watching the inauguration from London had their own issues. They were dealing with the wreckage created by the Brexit debate and the unfortunate and rushed trade talks with the European Union and others, exacerbated by the never-ending and serious spread of COVID-19, still without a fully proven and widely distributed vaccine, and the absence of a truly dominant UK political party. They had been hoping for discernable direction from the new president. But rather than articulating a detailed and cogent definition of the United States' foreign policy, the inaugural address presented the equivalent of a thousand-piece jigsaw puzzle with no detailed picture to go by.

A very similar discussion was taking place in Berlin, where it was an hour later. In that capital, the chancellor and foreign minister and their closest advisers watched the address together while maintaining a safe level of social distancing. Like the Brits, the Germans were intensely interested in how the new US administration saw its role in the world. Given the emergence of the post-Brexit European Union and developments in Asia, principally surrounding China, the United States would never return to the role it played prior to the Pope administration, much less prior to the Iraq War. But the United States was still needed as a counter to other lesser but dangerous powers and as an example of how democracy and capitalism can not only coexist but flourish together. And then there were the lingering effects of COVID-19 on health and the business climate throughout continental Europe, not to mention the issue of NATO's future.

Similar inconclusive assessments were taking place in places like Moscow, Beijing, Tokyo, New Delhi, Tehran, Jerusalem, Ankara, Paris, Brussels, Canberra, Ottawa, Brasilia, and Mexico City. The leaders of those governments, as well as pundits around the globe, were hopeful in some cases, worried in others, but in either case not at all sure why.

CHAPTER THREE

Back to Georgie's

After Margie's departure and listening to the inaugural address, Pepper felt the need to do anything but unpack. He decided to shave and shower. As he shaved in front of the mirror, he took stock of his 6'1" frame. He had put on weight since his wife's death, and he had been surviving on too much junk food. He still looked like he was in decent shape. However, he had not been exercising with any regularity. He needed to correct that before things got out of control. His dark hair, sprinkled with more and more gray as the months marched on, was getting shaggy by his standards. And the longer his hair, the more gray that showed.

Pepper still had coverage on his mobile phone, so he found Georgie's number and called to see if he could get an appointment for a haircut. Georgie himself answered the phone. Georgie must have had caller ID, and Pepper was calling with his mobile that had a 202 (DC) area code. Before Pepper could get a word in, Georgie hollered in the phone: "Hey, bub, nobody calls me from a 202 area code. I'm not interested in your survey, I ain't buyin' nothing, I don't need a car warranty or health insurance, and I don't donate nothin' to nobody. Don't call again."

Pepper virtually yelled into his phone as Georgie hung his up, "Hey, all I want is a haircut appointment." Pepper had the sense that

Georgie heard him, but he must have had too much momentum in slamming the phone down to be able to stop. So Pepper called back.

Georgie was still gruff. "You again, huh? Appointment? We don't make appointments. You come in, you take a number, you wait your turn in the shop or you do some shopping in the downtown area, and when your number comes up, you climb in the chair."

"Sorry," Pepper said. "I'm new in town and didn't know the rules."

"Ugh, newbies," Georgie grumbled. "Since you're new, if you want a haircut today, I'll give you number twenty-nine. I estimate that number will be up in about two hours at the end of the day. How's that work? Don't be late. What's your name?"

"Name is Pepper."

"That your first or last name?" Georgie asked. "Ah hell," he continued, "doesn't matter. The only peppers we have around here are grown in gardens. Are you comin' or not?"

"See you soon. Thanks," responded Pepper.

Pepper puttered around for a bit and then climbed in his somewhat elderly Volvo to drive into town. As he drove, he passed a sign with an arrow pointing straight ahead to the historical area. Carterville was a small town and county seat with a quaint downtown that included lots of two-story brick buildings dating from before World War II, brick sidewalks, a genuine town square with parking, trees and the prototypical courthouse, and many storefronts that at one time had windows providing a view into once-bustling shops. Sadly, they weren't so bustling anymore.

It was nearly dark outside when Pepper walked into the barbershop. On the wall were three sets of hooks that held numbers, a different color for each barber chair. Not much had changed in Georgie's barbershop since Pepper had had his going-away-to-college haircut. There was still a red, white, and blue barber pole outside. Indoors, the tin ceiling was still there, yellow from the days when patrons smoked at will. The linoleum floor, cast-iron barber chairs, big leather straps used to sharpen razors hanging down the side of the barber chairs, shave cream dispensers, and towel heaters were all without visible change. The shop was much bigger than needed for three barbers, and there were a lot of chairs, but many of them were stacked in a corner to allow for social distancing. Various out of date newspapers and magazines were in evidence, and there was a lot of chitchat going on. It was Inauguration Day after all.

One new feature was a large smart TV hanging on the wall, tuned to Fox News; another was the masks the barbers were all wearing. The use of masks by the customers was less uniform, but Pepper put his on.

The biggest difference in the shop was the barbers themselves. Georgie was Georgie, referred to by many customers as the "old white guy." But instead of three Caucasians, a second barber was a black male, and the third was a woman with brown skin. The customers were diverse, though a majority, like Georgie, were old white guys. It seemed like everyone in the shop was treated with equally good-natured disrespect in terms of reactions to their reviews of the president's speech—or anything else for that matter. But it also seemed that the chitchat avoided the most controversial issues. In that sense, it was a little like the discussion at the Thanksgiving table when the uncles and aunts and cousins were visiting and everyone avoided talking about politics.

"You must be number twenty-nine," Georgie said to Pepper. "Have a seat."

A number of the patrons looked like they had already had their haircut, but they hung around to, as Georgie later explained, "shoot the shit." Most of them were acquainted with one another, and most had opinions about the president's speech. Pepper was smart enough not to become an active participant in the banter. That allowed him to escape becoming a target. Besides, the people in the barbershop would figure out soon enough that he was from DC, and a lawyer to boot.

After Pepper was seated, Georgie turned the barber chair around so Pepper could see himself in the large mirror. He wasn't getting any younger. Apart from the gray hair, his face featured lines and a sort of ruddy complexion. Along with everything else going on in his life, Pepper was jolted a bit by his appearance. He just didn't think of himself as old. Maybe it was the lighting in the barbershop. But then there was the math.

Georgie interrupted this train of thought by asking, "What's your name, number twenty-nine?"

"Pepper," he said.

"That your first or last name?"

"Last."

"What name do you go by?"

"Hmm. Long story."

"That's okay," said Georgie. "We'll just call you Pepper."

"Well—let me try to give you the short version," offered Pepper. "My real first name is Staunton, I guess after a relative or the small town downstate where they hold the Shakespeare Festival. That got shortened to Stan among family members. When I was in high school, people still remembered the Beatles and started calling me Sarge after the song 'Sergeant Pepper's Lonely Hearts Club Band.' That didn't stick for very long, and people decided that Salt N. Pepper was a normal progression from Staunton Pepper. Then they started to use the obvious shorthand by calling me Salt. So a lot of people in the family call me Stan, and others who know me pretty well call me Salt."

"Got it," said Georgie. "Next time you come in, we'll figure out what to call you. Today, you're number twenty-nine. Are you new in town?"

"Yes and no," Salt responded. "I grew up and lived here till I went off to college. You cut my hair when I was in high school. People around here called our farm the Pepper Place. The Yoders lived there for a long time, and now that I'm retired, I'm thinking about moving back here."

"We heard there was a moving van out there," said Georgie. "People wondered what was going on. Where are you moving in from?

This was getting serious, and Salt said meekly, "Washington, DC."

"Well, son, what are you doing in this barbershop today?" Georgie asked. "Why aren't you at an inaugural party? You must have been one of those pointy-headed members of the Deep State. Or part of what we used to call the Trilateral Commission."

"Nope," Salt responded. "The truth is almost worse than that. For the past five years or so, I have been with a DC law firm, and before that, I worked in the Treasury Department and the State Department. But I'm getting over all of that."

"Good for you and welcome back," said Georgie. "I guess I'll just need to figure out how to give a pointy-headed haircut."

"You know," Salt said, "it's interesting that I haven't heard the words *Trilateral Commission* since I was in high school. I had an uncle who suspected that such a thing existed and that they secretly ran the US government if not the world. That was the reason he always kept a stash of gold and silver around as a hedge against who knows what. I later found out, to my surprise, that there actually was such a thing as the Trilateral Commission, and it included some powerful people. Today, I guess you would call them hedge fund managers, billionaires, business leaders, retired politicians, people who run huge political action committees, and other very bright people. Many of them show up at the World Economic Forum held in Davos, Switzerland once a year or in connection with Group of Seven or G-7 meetings; not many of them were ever elected. Not sure they did any harm in the old days. Still not sure they aren't a positive force."

"Well, there you go," said Georgie. "Seems like your uncle was mostly right."

Salt looked around the shop and decided he should try to reduce the outsider bias and introduce himself while Georgie was assembling his scissors and combs. He stood up and started walking around to chat, without shaking hands of course.

The first person introduced himself as Steve. "I farm here," he explained.

"What kind of farming?" Salt asked.

"Good question," responded Steve. "I used to be a grain and soybean farmer. But that was before President Pope double-crossed us and used tariffs to attack China. The Chinese reprisals hurt bad.

Then there was COVID-19 and our current recession. I don't know what I'll plant this spring, if anything. The grain markets are a mess. Sorry, but you asked."

"No problem," said Salt. "Sorry about the mess. I know that the tariff disruption lasted a long time, despite what President Pope said. And the recession has been Godawful."

"You are 100 percent correct," said Steve. "Right after I learned about tariffs, I had to learn about how hard it is to reengineer what they call supply chains, and then all hell broke loose with the pandemic and recession. Maybe I should do what everyone else around here seems to be doing and plant grapes, but I'm not sure folks are even buying wine these days. And it's hard to get excited about popping corks for the city folk and sippin' wine with them all day. No offense, of course."

"None taken." Salt next introduced himself to Roy. "What do you do, Roy?"

"I run the men's clothing store down the street—your typical small business trying to survive against Target, Walmart, the internet, and the recession."

"Good to meet you," Salt said. "After I get unpacked, I may need to come and see you."

"That would be great," offered Roy. "We'll take good care of you."

Next was Warren, one of the black patrons. "I work in the hardware store," Warren explained. "You being in the old Pepper place, you'll need what we have from time to time. Most our stuff is made in America. If you're looking for service, give us a try. You may need some handyman help, and we can recommend some. You need to know who's who around here. What with business going to hell last year, everyone and his brother is say'n' he's a handyman. Some can't drive a nail straight."

"Thanks," said Salt. "I imagine I'll be a regular customer for a while. And I'm not the most handy guy alive. That's a lawyer disease."

Finally, there was Don. "I don't do much since I retired," offered Don. "Just hoping that the government won't crash completely and take away my social security and Medicare."

"We're in the same boat, Don," said Salt. "Having just retired and counting on social security and Medicare, I also hope the government is careful."

"And by the way," volunteered Don, "I'm a hunter, a Second Amendment guy and a card-carrying member of the National Rifle Association. Just in case you wondered."

"Good to know. Thanks," replied Salt. "My dad was a member of the NRA, and I can still remember when we were in school here and got the first day of hunting season off from school. Do they still do that?"

"Not officially." Don smiled. "That would not be politically correct. But at least before COVID-19, we had the twenty-four-hour flu around here at certain times of the year. If you get my drift. Not sure what we'll do now. I guess the good news is that you don't have to worry about being six feet apart when walking in the woods with a bright orange jacket on."

By this time, it was nearing 5:45 p.m., and the other patrons, having had had their hair cut and knowing about Salt, started to leave. So did the other barbers.

After Don got through the door, he pulled a throwaway cell phone from his jacket pocket and dialed. When the other party answered, Don said, "It appears that a retired federale is moving into the Yoder family place. He seems to have been a civilian and was with the State Department. Does not seem to be FBI or Justice Department. Thought you might want to know."

The party on the other end of the call said simply, "Thanks. Sounds harmless enough, but let me now if you learn anything else interesting. And throw away this phone." Then Don heard nothing but the dial tone.

By the time Salt got back to the barber chair, it was just Salt and Georgie left in the barbershop. In these quiet few moments, Salt asked, "Georgie, this is a good place to get a haircut, but people clearly come in early and hang around before and after getting their cut. Why do you put up with that?"

"It's part of who we are. Most of the folks who hang around here work in town or are retired, semiretired, or unemployed; they have time on their hands, they don't belong to book clubs, there is only so much cable news you can take, and human interaction is a good thing. You didn't see it today, but they like to argue. They also like to get a bit of a shave and a hot towel. A number of these people are just plain lonely. And some are desperate. Talk about desperation, you should have been here last summer when it became obvious that the COVID-19 thing would hold on much longer and stronger than expected. Ugh. This shop was standing room only, and I had to take a few IOUs for haircuts. It was really sad—still is in a lot of cases.

"Anyhow, folks are welcome to hang around as long as I can stand on my aching feet. And they know the rules—the one here the longest leaves when the chairs get filled up and a new customer comes in."

Salt then asked, "How bad has the COVID-19 thing been around here? Did many people get it?"

"I think we had less than one hundred who got it last year and went to the hospital," responded Georgie. "They never did get the testing right, so nobody knows for sure. Something like fifteen died from it. Mostly older folks or people who had some other condition going on. But that damn virus has hung on like a dog with a favorite bone, and it is still in the air here and folks are still coming down with it. The health risk is really depressing. We really need that vaccine.

"You know, the illness was horrible, but the lockdown that people have had to sit through has also been really miserable, and we are still living with limitations on what we're supposed to do. With businesses closing or cutting back, many for good, people woke up to the fact that a lot of jobs were gone forever. You know, we lost a lot of stores here in the downtown area. I was lucky. I lost a lot of business, but at some point, people decide they need to get a haircut."

Georgie had started to cut Salt's hair, but Salt decided to press his luck. "None of my business, but do you have many women customers?"

"I don't," said Georgie, "but the other barbers do. If you're looking for a good cut and not two hundred dollars' worth of color and uppity styling, this is a good place for a woman to come. You didn't see any women here this afternoon because they tend to come in earlier and don't like some of the cursing that goes on later. Now, how do you want your hair cut?"

"Medium, I guess," responded Salt.

"Yeah, you look like a medium type of pointy-headed guy," Georgie said, laughing.

"One more question?" asked Salt.

"Okay, just one more," responded Georgie.

"What's with the Hair-i-Care sign behind you?"

Georgie laughed and handed Salt a piece of paper that said at the top "Hair-i-Care Application." Georgie got up on his soapbox: "All this talk about the green new deal and Medicare for all and forgiveness of college loans, and nothin', and I mean nothin', about controlling or subsidizing the cost of haircuts. So, we set up our own 10 percent discount program. But you have to apply and qualify."

Salt then focused on the application. It had seven questions:

> Hair-i-Care Application
>
> Name: _____
>
> 1. Are you a woman or a male with black or brown skin? If so, stop here. You qualify.
> 2. Are you sixty-five or older?
> 3. Have you had five of your last six haircuts here?
> 4. Have you volunteered anywhere during the past two months?
> 5. If you are a male and you used our restroom for #1, did you lift the seat? And then was your aim good so you hit the hole?
> 6. Have you shared with our customers a new, good, and reasonably clean joke during the past three months?
> 7. Have you mastered the art of directional farting?

Salt read them and laughed quietly, then asked who made the decisions as to who qualifies for a discount.

"Well," said Georgie, "I consult with the other barbers, and they get a vote, but I make the decisions, if you know what I mean."

"Got it," Salt responded. "But how about question number seven? Is that for real?"

"Hell yes," said Georgie, chuckling. "That's the polygraph question."

"Huh?"

"Anyone who answers that question yes is a liar and does not get the discount."

"Oaky." Salt laughed. "But how about number one? Seems to smack of affirmative action."

"Maybe," said Georgie. "We don't have long enough tonight to talk through that one. Just remember that this is one case where someone did what they thought was right in general terms and for their business, without any pushing or shoving from the government."

Since they were getting close to the topic, Salt asked, "How is the Black Lives Matter movement going here?"

Georgie thought for a few moments and responded, "Well, you ask a lot of questions, and now you're getting into touchy stuff. The truth is that the Black Lives Matter movement does not get a lot of play here. There were some mild demonstrations following the George Floyd killing in Minnesota but no violence. Hell, we don't have any statues to pull down even if a crowd wanted to do that. This is a small enough town that big crowds do not assemble for anything. Nobody buys into violence or riots, but a lot of people—all flavors of them—are beginning to understand that something is seriously wrong with our race relations. Most just don't talk much about it when strangers or people who don't get it are around. Next time you're here ask Max about this. That's his Black Lives Matter sign over there in the corner. He went to a couple demonstrations."

"Hmm," murmured Salt. "That must have been a controversial add to the barbershop."

"Not really," said Georgie. "Max is not just a black guy, he's Max. A person. People know him as a person and like him, even if they disagree with him about things like police brutality. Comfort comes more easily with the known than the unknown. Wasn't it a Secretary of Defense who used to talk about known knowns and known unknowns and the like? Besides, Max gives a good haircut."

Salt decided he would shut up and enjoyed the warm towel on his face after Georgie finished his haircut. Wisdom can be found in unusual places. It was good to be reminded of that.

CHAPTER FOUR

Life amid the Moving Boxes

The next day started out better. It felt like it must be warmer outside. The fog lifted, and Salt could see the mountains. *Why are they called the Blue Ridge?* he wondered. They looked a bit blue when the sunlight hit them the right way—or was he kidding himself? He had read somewhere that it was the chemistry of the soil affecting the tree leaves. But most of the leaves were gone. Well, not today's issue. The mountains were tranquil, relaxing, and majestic on their own, and that was welcome. To make things better, the sun had come out. It was not raining. This was not the Rockies as viewed from Denver or Boulder, but it was pretty damn good.

A few of Margie's chocolate chip cookies were left. The cookies were the only breakfast food he could find (though, truthfully, he didn't look very hard after finding the cookies), so he had several with two cups of coffee. So much for the good news; the boxes still remained.

Looking for inspiration, he found and connected the TV with some loose cables and a cable box that were on the floor and was surprised that the cable TV service was still on. Even better, the channel flipper was still on the floor near the cable box. He sat down with his coffee and cookies and flipped among Fox and Friends, CNN, Today, Good Morning America and MSNBC to get varying takes on the inauguration and the new president's address. Salt had lived in the District of Columbia all of his post–law school adult life but wasn't active in party politics as such. Like many of his government colleagues, he made a point of not voting when he was with the Treasury and State Departments. He avoided anything that looked, felt, or tasted like partisanship. He survived by being neutral and good at what he did. He had served under five presidents, and as he finished his government career with the State Department, he had become a jack-of-all-trades, handling tough issues in the background and developing trusted relationships. He had worked with both the more partisan players in the United States and key career diplomats overseas. People sought him out not for favors but for insight and judgment. He wasn't a person who liked to hear himself talk. But when he talked, people listened—at least some of the time.

Salt was by nature a moderate in style and thought—a person in the middle. He was either a moderate Republican or a moderate Democrat; nobody knew. He did vote in the most recent elections, and for the new president. But he did not view that as a close judgment call; it was more of an emergency response. He had gone through a major adjustment when he left the government and joined the law firm five years ago. He was again viewed as a seer, but he had to learn to be hyperresponsive to clients—and even to market a bit. During his first year out of the government, he was barred from lobbying directly, and that put a crimp in his style. He was sought out on all things international, was invited to join a company board (he declined, saying that he would rather represent them, and he did), and over time became moderately successful. But he was essentially an introvert, never got the hang of selling, and fundamentally remained a policy wonk.

Like most law firms, Salt's firm suffered during 2020 as the post-COVID-19 recession became more serious. There were cutbacks. Strangely, efforts to get back to expected normal in the fall of 2020 did not exactly head toward a familiar normal. The virus was not going away, and at the end of the year, they were still working on vaccines, with several in process and none fully approved and widely administered. Salt decided—probably mistakenly—after his wife, Meredith, died, that he needed to move on and would gracefully slide out of the law firm toward retirement at the end of the year. He wondered from time to time whether, despite Meredith's death, he would have been asked to retire even if he had not planned to do so. But he never had to find out. Probably just as well.

As Salt flipped among the news channels, he was keenly interested in the various and inconsistent takes on what the new president had said. Knowing that the president's words were important but that perception sometimes trumps reality, he paid attention across the broad commentator spectrum. Overall, he was pleased with the new president's words, as were most but not all of the commentators. But Salt knew that talk was cheap. He was also very aware that the senior career staff of the State Department had been decimated by the passage of time for baby boomers and by partisanship for others. The Pope administration had had three secretaries of state in four years and three sets of sycophant staffers to go with them. They would soon all be gone. There wasn't much wisdom to be passed along to their successors. The new president didn't have an overwhelming army of trusted professionals to deal with the results of the weaponization of foreign relations. And then there were the pandemic and recession that flashed signs of hope from time to time but were still significant problems. *Good luck, President Evans*, Salt thought as he finished his coffee, had one last cookie, and forced himself to go back to the boxes.

He started sorting boxes by floor—which meant carrying all manner of loads up an old and creaking staircase with ancient wallpaper on the walls and ceiling. That took until two o'clock in the afternoon. During that interval, he noticed that there seemed to be a lot of wallpaper all over the house. It was old and mostly one shade of green or another—in other words, ugly. Salt concluded that getting rid of the wallpaper and fixing the plaster issues that would almost certainly be uncovered if the wallpaper was taken down would be a major investment. Ditto the plumbing. After a short break for more coffee and cookies, he started sorting boxes room by room on each floor. He didn't get that task finished. By six o'clock, Salt had had it.

Coming around to the realization that the packers had not packed much of his food, Salt drove into town and stopped at the first fast-food joint he came to.

After a sumptuous meal of a cheeseburger and fries, Salt went home and watched an old cowboy movie on a cable channel that he had not known existed. He liked cowboy movies. They didn't force you to think; the good guys wore clean, light-colored hats and always won and got the girl, and the bad guys wore dirty dark hats and always lost. Cowboy movies were not particularly politically correct, especially on gender issues and as to Native Americans, but that was more than Salt could sort out that evening.

CHAPTER FIVE

Cutting Ties to the Past

Day three actually involved not only moving boxes but taking stuff out of them. This was not only hard work but also melancholy, as he found some of Meredith's things. That forced him to stop, go downstairs to sit on the couch, and think about his wife, her death, how much he missed her, and what to with her things. She was not only a spouse but also a best friend and confidante. He hadn't fully appreciated what a jewel she was until she was gone. He felt terrible that, because of the pandemic, it had not been possible to even have a proper memorial service for her. And, of course, the grief process was exacerbated by the fact that he was quarantined and isolated for several weeks after her death, and that was followed by weeks and weeks of working from home where he lived alone. He was miserable and lonely and just wanted to get the hell out of the apartment.

Several counselors had urged him to deal with his wife's things long before this. That was good advice but a road not taken. Now, tears that had not previously been shed flowed freely down his cheeks. After an hour of quiet sobs and introspection, he concluded that, for better or worse, he needed to move on, and keeping his wife's wardrobe in a closet of an old farmhouse would be like inviting ghosts in to play. She would not approve.

What do to with her clothes? Donate them obviously—but where?

The Wi-Fi wasn't yet hooked up in the farmhouse, so his internet access was limited to his phone. Rather than relying on his mobile, he looked for and somehow found the scrap of paper with Margie Hatcher's phone number on it and called her for advice. It was an awkward call, but she was very helpful. Armed with Margie's advice and encouragement, he loaded the boxes full of his wife's clothes in his Volvo (it took two loads) and delivered them to the thrift shop run by several of the local churches.

This made him feel both worse and better. But that seemed to be the way the week was going.

Salt had not taken a shower since the move, and he felt grimy as well as whipped. The movers had packed some soap and shampoo, and much to his delight, he found that the water in the bathtub worked. And it was hot. There was no shower—there was only an old cast-iron tub with a hose he could use to wash his hair. It felt good enough, and Salt thought maybe he was getting close to rejoining the human race. About time.

CHAPTER SIX

Getting to Know Margie

Rejoining the human race involved eating something other than cookies and cheeseburgers. Salt put on some clean clothes and decided to try Helen's Place, the diner recommended by Margie.

Salt drove into town and walked into Helen's after reading the sign on the front door, now required by law, saying that all of Helen's employees had been tested for COVID-19 within the past two weeks, had their temperatures taken when they came to work for the day, and were required to wear masks. Patrons were also warned not to move the furniture, which was set up in compliance with the current and ever-changing social distancing requirements for indoor food service.

Helen's was clean and orderly but not fancy. It was a sort of Silver Diner–looking kind of place, but the booths, napkin holders, jukeboxes, and utensils were genuine rather than faux old. Salt thought the same could be said of the diner's staff.

Salt got a booth and asked if he could order a drink. The diner had no hard liquor and only local Virginia wines—some of which were actually pretty good. He ordered the red Helen sold by the glass, a side salad (Meredith would have approved), and the meat loaf. He learned that he was being served by Helen herself, so Salt introduced himself. The diner wasn't busy, allowing Salt to chat with Helen, who turned out to be a character. It was lucky that Salt was a good listener. She detailed for Salt the effects of the COVID-19 virus and the recession, the painful layoffs Helen had to do, how close Helen got to closing up, and the time she threw the keys on the table in front of the landlord, explaining that he could take over the damn diner if he wanted, but she was not paying any more rent until she could open up. She was still hurting financially and very tired of wearing a mask.

As he sat there thinking about Helen's comments, Margie Hatcher walked in. She saw him and walked over. "How are you doing?" she asked. "I know from our call you had a tough day."

"I did, but I think I've worked my way through it," said Salt. "Thanks again for your help." Salt realized that she was still standing and asked if she would care to join him.

"I would be glad to, but I don't want to intrude," Margie responded.

Salt smiled. "The only thing you would be interrupting is the sound of silence." Margie sat down a safe distance away and ordered a glass of white, and they exchanged small talk, including some about politics. Salt followed his policy of talking politely about politics in general while actually saying very little about his. He got the impression that, like himself, Margie did not advertise it but was somewhere in the middle of the political spectrum.

They shared a bit more about their backgrounds. "What kinds of things did you do when you were with the Treasury Department?" she asked.

"Well, most of it was pretty boring now that I look back on it. I spent a couple of years in the Treasury Department's Office of Foreign Asset Control, better known as OFAC," explained Salt. "One of its functions is to define and administer US sanctions programs. Those programs take advantage of the relative strength of the US economy and the broad reach of our financial institutions and markets. Essentially, the government, through OFAC, can prohibit so-called US persons—a very broadly defined term—from engaging in transactions or trade with a country, a business, or a person. Over the years, that has included countries like Cuba, Iran, Russia, Syria, North Korea, and the like."

"That sounds pretty complicated," said Margie. "Isn't there a risk that countrywide sanctions have unintended consequences for the innocent?"

"Fair comment," said Salt. "In more recent years, OFAC has become more targeted and, rather than going after countries all of the time, has sometimes focused on particular entities and individuals that US persons are not permitted to deal with. For some of the targeted Specially Designated Individuals, as we called them, this produced a world of hurt. They ran the risk of having tied up in knots big sums of money that touched banks doing business in the United States. They would retain advisers to try to get them out of the target zone, and some US persons would try to get licenses that would allow them to do particular types of business with a sanctioned party. That's also the sort of thing I worked on when I was with the law firm."

Salt finished, "Well, that concludes a short course on part of my career. I warned you. Pretty boring."

"I would say it's complicated and interesting but not boring," responded Margie. "Did the sanctions work?"

"What I'm about to say is a personal view only," cautioned Salt. "The answer is yes and no. Did it change Iran's foreign policy? Some but not so much. Did it punish people trying to do business with Iran and therefore indirectly penalize Iran? Yes."

The conversation then drifted in Margie's direction. Salt was a better listener than a talker, and he learned quite a bit about Margie. He wondered why, after five years, she had not remarried. Maybe, like him, she was still in love with her spouse and just could not get over it.

It was good to have some casual human interaction. Salt could not remember the last time that had happened with anyone, male or female. For the first time, during dinner, Salt noticed things that went below Margie's surface attractiveness. She was smart, informed, well-read, fun, a volunteer for good causes, and pretty in her own way, with medium-length auburn hair, brown eyes, and a strong chin line. She clearly took good care of herself. She also made great chocolate chip cookies.

And she was just plain nice. At the end of dinner, Margie offered to have him over to her place for some home cooking if he was interested. "Sound's great," he replied, surprising himself with his swift response.

"I'm having some friends over for dinner next week. I think you could tolerate them, and they're sure to be interested in the newcomer who is actually a native of the area." She wrote down the address, date, and time and handed it to him.

At home and after going to bed, Salt tried to remember the last time he had actually had a meaningful discussion with a woman. His mind was blank on that subject, but he knew he had not been to bed with a woman since long before Meredith died. None of this helped him sleep. He added to his to-do list, next to his bed, buying some sleeping pills and going to the liquor store.

CHAPTER SEVEN

Beltway Beckons

Day four started uneventfully. More boxes, more donations to the church thrift store, more memories, and a better understanding of what an old farmhouse would require in the way of modernizing. It was daunting but nothing compared to the call he got on his mobile around ten thirty in the morning.

The call was from Stuart Bacon, who the news reports had named as a likely pick for secretary of state or a comparable position, in terms of influence, in the West Wing of the White House. Maybe director of national intelligence, another cabinet-level position that oversaw the US intelligence community, including the Central Intelligence Agency, the National Security Agency, and others. Salt knew and respected Stuart as a thoughtful guy who had survived in several cages full of politicos. Even more impressive was his sustained diplomatic service under several presidents in an era of extreme political turbulence. Stuart was a survivor without the level of baggage that normally accompanied that tag.

"To what do I owe the honor of this call, Stuart?" asked Salt. "And before you go any further, congrats on being wherever and whatever you are. I wasn't sure that people of your quality could survive these days. It's one of the few recent developments that I find comforting."

"Thanks, Salt. That means a lot coming from you," responded

Stuart. "This is a busy time, so I'll get to the point. We would like to pick your brain, and to that end, we'd like you to come into DC for a meeting on Monday afternoon at the White House. The meeting would be with me and one or two others. Probably not the president, though the president knows I'm making this call and why. We have a lot of bridge building to do with lots of people, including alienated allies, if there is such a thing, and we need your thoughts about how to go about that."

Salt was shocked and took several seconds to settle himself. He had no clue that he would get a call of this nature. "Thanks, Stuart," said Salt, "but I've been out of the game for five years. I'm a dinosaur when it comes to this sort of thing. And if the president or the president's supporters thought much about my views, they would have asked during the campaign." Salt didn't add that he probably would not have answered a call from a political campaign.

"Salt, the fact that you have been out of the game, as you put it, is one of several reasons we're calling," explained Stuart. "Not much good happened while you were gone. You don't have recent baggage. And you have perspective, which is important. You're also well respected, both here and abroad. You may not be a unicorn, but you're in that family. All we're asking is that you make a trip into DC and sit down with us. You owe the country that much."

Salt hesitated for a moment, knowing that there was likely more going on here than met the eye. But he could hardly refuse. He said it: "Okay, but all I'm agreeing to is one meeting that will almost certainly disappoint you."

"Great," Stuart replied. "The guards will expect you around 1:30 p.m., and bring some ID. You know the drill. And thanks. By the way, will this mobile number I called work for the next few days in case we need to move things?"

"Yep," said Salt, "at least until the Russians bring down our telecommunications systems."

"How about email?" asked Stuart.

"You can text me on my phone, but I don't have internet here yet.

Don't send anything that's very long. I'm getting used to no email attachments. See you Monday."

Later in the day, Salt got a voice mail message from Stuart suggesting that since the meeting was not until Monday afternoon, it would be helpful for Salt to stop by the CIA on his way down the George Washington Parkway into DC and meet with Louise Roseaux to start the process of getting his security clearance updated. Salt had no intention of doing anything that required a clearance update. The move to the farm had not been an overwhelming success so far, but it had not been a complete disaster either, and it was early. Salt ignored the message from Stuart and the one that came in later in the day from Ms. Roseaux.

CHAPTER EIGHT

Enter Louise

Salt drove back into the dreaded DC traffic on Monday morning, allowing plenty of time for delays. He hated traffic—even the slightly lower volume that the remnants of the COVID-19 lockdown and recession had brought about—but at least today it beat unpacking moving boxes. Fortunately, the weather was cooperating. Although overcast, there was no precipitation. Out of spite, Salt did not drive down the George Washington Parkway past the CIA, instead taking Interstate 66 all the way onto the Roosevelt Bridge and Constitution Avenue. He was late enough that he avoided the rush hour toll. The drive gave Salt time to think in the quiet—and without the distraction of what still seemed like hundreds of remaining boxes—about what this meeting could really be about. He had no idea.

As he pulled into the White House, he momentarily panicked, thinking he had forgotten his briefcase. Then he recalled that he didn't bring one. It was hard to imagine walking into a meeting in the West Wing without a briefcase, or with an empty one. The outdoor guards asked what he was carrying. "Nothing other than my keys, wallet, and mobile," Salt responded. Their eyebrows went up quizzically and screamed doubt and uncertainty. That in itself almost made the trip worthwhile.

As he checked in with security inside the White House, one

of the officers told him that Mr. Bacon had left a message that the meeting would need to start about an hour late, but the guard had been instructed to call Ms. Roseaux, who would greet Salt and meet with him during the delay. The inside security guards asked if he wanted a mask but didn't force him to wear one since he had a certificate confirming that he had recently been tested for COVID-19, but they took his temperature with a fancy electronic gun. Sensing that the new administration had a different view of masks than the Pope administration, Salt took the mask. They asked again about his briefcase, and Salt was delighted to say again that he didn't have one. Then they forced him to deposit his mobile phone with them. It was five years old and a bit of an embarrassment. But life went on. And he still missed his Blackberry.

Having no real choice, Salt went with Ms. Roseaux into a small, barren room in the West Wing. She was tall, trending toward skinny but muscular, dressed in a severe black pantsuit, with midlength black hair worn straight. Her skin was dark enough that she might be the product of some mixing and matching. Whatever, it worked, even with the mask on. And she was very proper and polite. "We're sorry about the delay, but we can put the time to good use if you're willing to give me an update on matters relating to your security clearance, which has expired under the terms of President Pope's 2019 revocation of the security clearances of former senior intelligence personnel."

"But I have no intention of needing a security clearance," said Salt.

"I'm sorry, Mr. Pepper, but the nature of the meeting you are here for is such that you cannot attend very much of it unless I believe you are eligible for the highest level of security clearance. This won't be a wasted effort, even if nothing comes of the meeting."

"Are you attending the meeting, Ms. Roseaux?" asked Salt.

"Yes," she responded.

"Can you tell me what it's about?" asked Salt.

"No."

"Do you know what it's about?"

"Only on a superficial basis," she responded.

Salt continued a bit more harshly: "Would you kindly tell me what you know about the meeting?"

"I understand your frustration, but you'll soon learn," she calmly explained. "In the meantime, let's not further delay the meeting. As I said, I need to preliminarily clear you before you can be told about the meeting or participate in it. Surely you're curious."

"Okay, but this is nuts. Kindly note my objection." Salt was huffing and puffing through his mask.

Salt spent the next hour responding to Louise's endless checklist of questions and describing his activities since leaving the government five years ago, his personal and law firm business dealings, his finances, who he regarded as friends (a short list), his drinking habits, his gender preference, details as to his travel outside of the United States, and his contacts outside of the United States. For once, it was good to be boring.

Toward the end of the session, he asked Ms. Roseaux, "So, who are you? What's your background? Why are you going to be in this meeting?"

"That's classified at a very high level." She smiled, not warmly.

Then they finally got the call to come into the meeting.

CHAPTER NINE

Selling Salt at the White House

They moved into a larger and more formal but still nondescript conference room in the West Wing and were soon joined by Stuart Bacon and his assistant, Alex. After abbreviated small talk and introductions, Stuart began the discussion by emphasizing that what was said in the room needed to stay there, with the exception of briefing the president.

Stuart opened. "Salt, as you can imagine, we have spent a massive amount of time and effort assessing our diplomatic relations since the election. Those efforts have been hindered by the litigation over the election results and boorish lack of cooperation from the Pope team. Nevertheless, we have been identifying candidates to assume positions of significant responsibility in the intelligence agencies, internationally oriented slots at Treasury, ambassadorships, and of course positions with the State Department. I will be either the secretary of state or here in the White House as director of national intelligence.

"We have been consulting with friends and foes about what the issues are and what our staffing should look like. Frankly, things are worse than we imagined. Our foreign relations are very troubled. They were bad before the COVID-19 pandemic, worse as the pandemic and recession took hold, and now look like a very troubled enterprise. We still have some very talented people in the diplomatic corps, but we have also lost a host of good people to firings, retirement, and disgust with the last administration. The good people still here will need to stretch and grow in their responsibilities. Many of them can. But we need reinforcements."

"Let me stop you there, Stuart," said Salt. "For a host of reasons, I'm not the right person to be serving as a reinforcement. If that's what you have in mind, we can call time-out now."

"That's not exactly what we have in mind," responded Stuart. "Let me finish. As you know, the United States has suffered significantly diminished credibility, whether dealing with friend or foe. We are variously viewed as volatile, xenophobic, racist, withdrawn, self-absorbed, unreliable, and untrustworthy. The lack of trust is deep and a serious problem. We have reluctantly concluded that people viewed as political appointees, or otherwise closely allied with the new administration, will not be as effective as in the past. At least in the near term, what they say to others in the world will often be treated as just more blah, blah, blah—and only good for as long as that person is around, at best.

"How do we fight this? With a new and very closely held approach. We need investigation and guidance from someone who is not viewed as political poison and, more important, has a reputation among the career diplomats in other countries for being trustworthy and able to maintain confidences. Someone who views Twitter, Facebook, and Instagram as the enemy and never to be used. In other words, we need a friendly dinosaur from those days of yesteryear when looking someone in the eye meant something. We need this dinosaur to consult with the trusted core of the diplomatic structure of other major countries—outside of the pressures created by publicly announced positions and the media—and then report back, on a very high and sensitive level, his or her findings and recommendations."

Stuart continued, "What are the issues of most importance? What do they need to see from us? What treaties can or need to be patched back together? What makes sense in that regard for the United States as well as others? Can we salvage existing alliances and create new ones? Apart from attacking even more aggressively the continuation of the coronavirus pandemic and fighting the recession, what do the priorities need to be?

"We would give you a short list of priority targets. We think the consultations need to start with the UK, but to a large extent, you would actually control your own agenda and priorities, with periodic reports back, both as needed and per a schedule.

"You would essentially be your own boss and report directly to me and the president. There would be no Senate confirmation. We would brief the leaders of key congressional committees as to what you're up to, but you would not be scheduled for public appearances.

"You would be a troubleshooter and a diplomatic relations turnaround specialist. Should be a great challenge and an incredibly important service to the country." Stuart paused.

"You've got to be kidding," responded Salt. "What you're describing here is not mission impossible, it's mission suicide. It won't work. And I'm the wrong guy to try. I am virtually anonymous. This is nuts. Did you find this in a bad book or a worse movie? What did I do to you to deserve this kind of thing? Come on, man!"

"Well, tell me what you really think." Stuart sighed. "And by the way, thanks for not saying no in the middle of that blast. At least you understand the degree of difficulty here. But what a great capstone for a career this could be. I would be tempted to do this myself, but I'm too politicized. On the other hand, you have a low profile and could pull it off. You would be surprised how often we've had positive reactions to the mention of your name in some discussions with allies about this initiative."

Salt growled. "You mean you cleared this with others before even mentioning it to me? What the hell, Stuart?"

"Well, Salt," Stuart said calmly, "we could hardly sell it to you and then be told by key allies that you're a nonstarter. Admittedly, some allies were more enthusiastic than others. And we ran a few other names through in addition to yours. Some people may have thought you were a placebo of sorts, but the reactions were neutral at worst, and a number were enthusiastic. There is a hunger across the world for a United States that is rational and trustworthy and willing to lead. You won't have trouble lining up meetings, even with those who were ambivalent."

"And how would the nutcase who takes this job get things done in terms of support?" Salt asked. "Most people like me have no infrastructure. I have no entourage and don't want one."

"We will of course provide support," Stuart explained. "We don't see this as being a big team. You have met Ms. Roseaux, whose real name will remain secret for the time being. She has been with the CIA in several roles, speaks French, Arabic, and Russian, knows who's who at the Agency and State, and believes in this cause. Her parents were French and American."

Stuart continued, "I think you need to think about this a bit more before we go any further. Admittedly, this is not an obvious next career step for someone in your situation. Why don't we call it a day and allow you two to get together over the next few days to discuss next steps. But time is not on our side."

As if on cue, the door opened, and the president's head partially popped through. "Thanks, Salt, for thinking about this. We need your help." And then the president disappeared before anyone could stand up or say anything.

Salt knew he had to nip this in the bud. "Look, Stuart, this may seem ungrateful, but there's nothing to think about; I just moved out to the edge of the Blue Ridge, for God's sake."

Stuart wasn't taking no for an answer. "All we ask is that you and Ms. Roseaux get together and discuss it. I'm sure she would be glad to come out to see you. If we can't get you, at least tell us how you would do this, or something like it. Thanks, Salt."

Stuart left abruptly and flashed a thumbs-up on his way out. As Salt left the White House, Louise gave him an encrypted phone for use in connection with this project and her phone number for "temporary use." She said she could come out to see him any day that week. Salt said she should aim for Thursday and warned that his farmhouse looked like it had been hit by a tornado.

"I'll be there at one o'clock." She smiled. "No lunch needed."

CHAPTER TEN

Small Town America Issues I

Tuesday was the date of Margie's dinner party. Prior to taking a shower and finding in his collection of boxes a sport coat to wear, Salt spent the day thinking about his meeting at the White House, what they said they wanted, what they really wanted, what they probably really needed, and how to get out of further discussions of this. The challenges and opportunities that Stuart outlined were real, but Salt didn't see himself as being what the doctor ordered. And he was tired, both mentally and physically. This was not what he had signed up for. Come to think of it, he didn't sign up for anything. How did this happen?

He arrived at Margie's smallish single-family home a polite ten minutes after 6:00 p.m. Salt wasn't the first to arrive, but he was not the last either. Margie answered the doorbell, opening the door and greeting him. "Glad you could make it, Salt. I am pleased to be able to introduce you to some good and interesting friends." She then took his temperature with one of the new-fangled electronic thermometers and confirmed that Salt was okay. She also commented that they would not be violating the maximum of ten persons rule and would do their best on social distancing. Margie also delicately asked if Salt needed or wanted a mask. He saw that others were not wearing masks and didn't want to look like the Lone Ranger, especially since his temperature was normal, so he declined.

Margie first introduced Salt to Mary and George Anderson. Mary was president of the largest local bank, Carterville Community Bank. It seemed that George, who was less outgoing, was an entrepreneur of sorts who also did some teaching on the side. Both George and Mary were obviously very smart. They had two teenagers getting close to college age.

Also interesting was Alan Greene, the president of Carterville University, and his partner, Angelo. They did not mention any kids. Despite its name, the university was fundamentally a well-regarded liberal arts college. The *university* designation came from the fact that the school offered graduate degrees in teaching. Both Alan and Angelo were very outgoing. Salt missed what Angelo did for a living. Alan was black, and his scholarship was in history, with a focus on post–Civil War reconstruction. He had very interesting perspectives on the Black Lives Matter movement and related topics.

Bob and Betty Reardon were a bit more reserved than the others. Bob owned the local GM dealership ("Come and see me if you need a good deal on a pickup for use on the farm"), and Betty stayed very busy with four kids and activities at the local Catholic church.

One other couple associated with Margie's book club or the Methodist church she attended was also there. Never good with names, Salt did not pick up theirs, but they were not handing out business cards either.

Given the proximity of the inauguration and the continuing impact of the recession and the Black Lives Matter movement, the discussion over a very tasty and healthy salmon dinner inevitably turned to politics and related topics. The dialogue was naturally awkward as the other guests tried to figure out where in the political spectrum Salt stood and how he voted, all without asking directly. Nobody wanted to ignite the equivalent of a family fight. Salt finally acknowledged, "I know everyone is wondering, given my background in what President Pope used to call the swamp, what my politics are. It's pretty unexciting. When I worked at the Treasury and State Departments, I didn't vote. I just thought it was better to be apolitical. In some senses, that hurt me I'm sure, but it also saved me in others. This most recent election was the first presidential election in many years that I have voted in—since I was then out of government—and I voted for President Evans. I'm basically a boring middle-of-the-roader."

"There! I told you, you would not get anything out of him," Margie exclaimed as she passed the salad. "You really have to squeeze things out of him." Everyone chuckled politely.

"Well," said Mary Anderson, who was clearly ready to unload on someone, "as a banker, I'm curious about your views on the recession, the massive business loan programs initiated last year, and the direction of interest rates. Bank stocks have struggled since early last year, and we bankers go crazy with rate volatility, which can cut either way at the bottom line. President Pope badgered the Federal Reserve to the point where they lowered interest rates effectively to zero last year, and they have not recovered. This means, first, that we can't be comfortable with the independence of the Fed; second, that there is very little dry powder left if we need to do more from a monetary standpoint; and third, that it is very hard for banks to make money these days. We went from an inverted, or nearly inverted, yield curve to the point where the yield curve is almost irrelevant. Ugh. And of course, thanks to President Pope's first tax cut and the massive recession relief, the federal deficit has exploded."

"I'm glad to share my thoughts on those subjects," said Salt, "but these are only my views, and they're not worth much. And I'm no economist. Of course, neither was President Pope. I have no idea whether lowering interest rates and the other significant steps taken by the Fed and the Treasury starting in the spring of 2020 were the right things to do. Something had to be done to pull the economy out of a self-induced coma, that's for sure. It's still too early to tell, though the stock market seems to think things are once again headed in the right direction. I do know that creating doubt as to the independence of the Fed is a very bad thing. It diminishes the reputation of the Fed and makes it much harder for people here and abroad to give the Fed the benefit of the doubt. I'm concerned that we may no longer be in a position to lead interdependent international efforts to stabilize the global economy. Instead of leading, we're just part of the pack."

"I can assure you that, despite all the government has done, things have not recovered," commented Bob, the GM dealer. "I have a lot full of 2020 and 2021 vehicles that I need to sell. And so do all of my competitors. The government is not bailing out the auto industry—unless you think converting auto factories into ventilator manufacturers is the answer."

The talk of ventilators did not add to the ambiance of the evening, but Margie nonetheless passed again the salmon, wild rice, and green beans as the chatter continued.

Responding to Bob, Salt said, "I guess the only good news is that you have been able to borrow at very low rates from Mary's bank, partially under the special small business loan programs that were rolled out last year."

"Well," said Mary, "we still have low inflation, and the job numbers are slowly recovering, but manufacturing and GDP growth are very soft, nobody is investing in the future because they can't, and the level of uncertainty on myriad issues is limiting growth in all kinds of ways. People are hurting, and it doesn't help that we're viewed by many foreigners as cowboys from the Wild West. Like it or not, our economy is part of a global economy, and we need to be meaningful players—well, actually the global leader—in that area."

"I'll say it's a mess," piped in Bob. "Our farmers around here— even little old Carterville—depend on being in a cross-border market that works. Pope and his tariffs on China, the backlash against our farm products, and the recession are not helping me sell new pickups to farmers with grain to haul. All of us feel this."

"Right," said Mary. "Without getting into names, I can tell you that there are more than a few farmers around here losing sleep over how to get through another year. It's sad, and their bankers are also stressed." With that, the guests finally focused on the main course.

"So, you're saying that things international directly affect both the business and mood of relatively remote financial ecosystems like the Carterville area?" asked Salt as Margie and others cleared the main course dinner plates.

"Absolutely," said Alan Greene, the college president. "I'll give you more examples. At a time when clear demographic trends reduce the number of prospective college students in the United States, the recession exacerbates affordability issues, and many in the middle and lower classes are questioning the cost and value of a college education, we are offending non-US governments and families who have sent their students to us. Many of those students can't get visas. And we're struggling to provide needed greater levels of financial aid to domestic students. All of this mush about free college and forgiveness of student loans that became standard progressive fare during the presidential campaign circuit will never happen, but the chatter has an effect. Sometimes perception is reality—at least for a while. This is all on top of the government passing a tax bill in 2017 that doesn't help the needy very much but does hurt the level of charitable contributions because they're not deductible by those who standardize. I could go on, but you can understand why we see things as being very interdependent. You don't need to be an economist to figure this out, but we have them at the college, and they have."

"How is your enrollment holding up?" Salt asked.

"Oh my," Dr. Greene replied. "The reality is we don't know from semester to semester. Parents remain concerned about things like adequate COVID-19 testing, kids living in dorms and eating in large dining halls, and whether we will have to go back to being virtual. We're holding our breath to see how many students actually show up for the second semester, which we have delayed a few weeks to give more time for the disease to be more fully eradicated. We certainly do need a fully tested vaccine."

Margie saved the day with a cold chocolate dessert of some kind. "Maybe," Salt commented, "we need a pause in this discussion so we don't allow this great dessert to melt entirely! We haven't even gotten to sanctions and the direction of the coronavirus."

All agreed and turned to lighter dinner chatter, mellowed a bit by the consumption of dessert and more wine.

At the end of the evening, Salt was one of the last to leave. "I hope you weren't offended by being in the target zone all evening," said Margie.

"No, I actually enjoyed myself," Salt said. "Everyone was both polite and interesting, and I learned some things. Besides, the food was great, and it was nice to see what an organized home looks like. I owe you a dinner, but we'll have to go out. I don't cook, and you know I don't unpack or clean."

"I would enjoy that." Margie smiled. "There are some nice country inns in the area where you can have a good dinner. And I won't pepper you with questions."

"Good," responded Salt. "It won't happen right away, as I may have some travel in my near future, but you have a rain check—one that works without the need to have rain."

CHAPTER ELEVEN

Farming in the New Normal

The next morning, Salt woke up in a good but thoughtful mood and started the day with two cups of coffee and no cable news blaring. He had been surprised by the level of sophistication among the dinner party participants, and a bit by the strength of their continuing unease. The views of real people from outside the Beltway were both refreshing and enlightening. It was clear, from both those at dinner and among Georgie's barbershop patrons, that people were not at ease with their government, regardless of where they were on the political spectrum. They had become less interested in fireworks than trustworthiness. Maybe the Democrats were smart in not allowing the party to drift too far to the left. Salt's take was that most of the Carterville folks he had met were slightly to the right of center. They had not wanted to vote again for President Pope, but they damn sure had not been looking for revolutionaries either.

Salt's thoughts were interrupted by a knock on the back door. He thanked goodness he had gotten dressed when he woke up.

Jack Davis, Salt's new tenant farmer, was at the door. Jack asked

Salt if he had a few minutes, and Salt was glad to oblige and poured coffee for each, bringing Salt up to three cups.

"Sorry to bother you, Salt," said Jack, "but I'm in a bind and need to be honest with you, especially with you moving out here and all."

"Sorry to hear that, Jack. How can I help?" responded Salt.

"Terminate our lease on the farm."

Salt sat quietly for a few moments, trying not to look as stunned as he was. "Wow, Jack. Our lease is less than a year old, and I tried to be very fair with you. What's the problem?"

Jack sighed. "It's complicated, but the short version is that farming doesn't work anymore as a way for the little guy to make a living. When you're losing money on every bushel of grain you grow, you can't make it up in volume. When we entered into our lease in late 2019, I thought I could make it by, in effect, spreading my fixed costs over a larger number of acres. That should have worked, but the market just plain sucks. Things were bad before the COVID-19 thing, and now even worse because of the virus shutdown, the recession and a trade war I don't understand. What I do understand is that I can't continue like I have. I need to farm the acres I own and do the best I can, and find another job to cover the shortfall. I won't have time to farm your 150 acres, and even if I did, that would only make things worse, unless of course you want to pay me to farm your land."

After some fast thinking, including around that fact that he needed someone to look after whatever was in the barn, Salt asked, "Assume for the sake of discussion that the grain market improves. Would you want to lease the farm again?"

"Depending on the lease terms and the market, yes," said Jack. "But those are big ifs."

Salt toughened up a bit. "You know, Jack, that I don't have to let you out of the lease. But I was to get a share of the profit, and it's not such a big deal if there is no profit. But if I let you off the hook, I'd be doing you at least a minor favor."

"I get that," said Jack, "and believe me, I don't like to come asking for favors. I was awake all night thinking about this discussion. I'm a man of my word. But at the same time, marching into bankruptcy is sort of a crazy strategy. And you know that's likely a lose-lose proposition."

"And I get that as well," replied Salt. "Here's my proposition. We'll suspend the lease of my farm to you for one growing season—say until October 31, 2021. At that time, we will reassess and either put the lease into effect for 2022, terminate it, or change the deal somehow. In exchange for my agreeing to do that, you will maintain the barn and the equipment out there. If you need to go out of pocket to do that, we'll discuss what it costs on an item-by-item basis, and I'll cover the agreed-upon cost. Finally, we will keep this discussion confidential."

"That's more than fair and okay by me." Jack smiled. "Do we need something in writing on this?"

"I'm fine if we shake hands on it—or these days touch elbows or bow to each other," said Salt. "If you want to get a lawyer, that's fine by me, and maybe you should since I'm a lawyer, but I would rather work this out between neighbors. And even though you're here walking out on our deal, I'm prepared to trust you."

"Works for me," confirmed Jack, who then continued: "Salt, you're from Washington and a lawyer. Can you help me understand how these tariffs on stuff to and from other countries are supposed to work? Even forgetting the effects of the recession, the tariff battle with the Chinese is killing a lot of farmers in this country, and once those markets get screwed up, trying to get them back in working order is nigh unto impossible."

"I'm happy to try, but they can work in lots of variations and are not entirely simple, and then there's the theory and the reality," said Salt.

Salt then explained, "Let's assume that country A has a state-controlled economy and a surplus of certain metal products and decides to get rid of it in the United States by lowering the price to below the cost of manufacturing. One approach by those in the United States hurt by this type of conduct would be to accuse country A of what is called dumping—that is, dumping cheap metal products on the market, which hurts US metal products producers but helps

US buyers of metal products. Assuming country A is party to a trade treaty with the United States or is one of the 164 members of the World Trade Organization, the United States might file a dumping complaint with the World Trade Organization. Or the United States might decide that would take too long and might or might not result in relief from the dumping. Instead, the United States might assert a 'national security' exception to trade treaty dispute processes and take things into its own hands and impose a tariff on the metal products sold in the United States by country A.

"The tariff in effect increases the price of country A metal products sold in the United States and in theory levels the playing field in an effort to persuade country A to stop trying to dump the metal products in the United States at artificially low prices. But it operates like a tax on US buyers of the metal products."

"Where does the grain come in?" asked Jack.

Salt continued, "In response to the US tariff on metal products, country A might reciprocate by imposing a tariff on other goods, like grain, sold by US producers to buyers in country A. The tariff sort of levels the playing field by offsetting country A's reduced volume of sales of low-price metal products with a reduction in the volume of grain bought by purchasers in country A. Country A understands the linkage.

"So the tariffs in effect hurt US grain farmers and country A buyers of grain, and hurt country A sellers of metal products and some US buyers of metal products, and help some US producers of metal products, and can result in multiple rounds of reciprocal tariffs or other countermeasures."

"Ugh," commented Jack. "Feels like a lot of unintended consequences here at home in the good old USA."

"You're getting the picture," commented Salt. "There are several problems with all of this. First, as a practical matter, the metal products tariff may or may not dissuade country A from dumping the metal products. Second, US buyers of the metal products in our example will in effect pay the tariff imposed by the United States through increased prices, so it feels like a tax. Third, country A may decide to impose counter-tariffs on other goods from the United States—like farm products—resulting in what is loosely called a trade war. Finally, country A might decide to offset the tariffs by manipulating its currency pricing against the US dollar so the price of metal products in US dollars in effect goes down and offsets the tariff."

"Okay," said Jack. "I get that in general terms, I think, but it's complicated, and I'm not sure what's going on here."

"Fair enough," said Salt. "So, let's get closer to home. Assume, for example, that country A buys a lot of wheat from the United States, in effect from farmers like you. Country A engages in activities, such as stealing US intellectual property, that the United States wants to discourage. The United States then decides to try to change country A's behavior by imposing tariffs, roughly equal to a reasonable licensing fee, on selected country A goods such as consumer electronics that are imported into the United States from country A. Country A reciprocates by either cutting back on its purchases of US wheat or imposing a combination of tariffs and quotas on US wheat, in either case hurting the United States but more directly the farmers who have benefitted from the sales to country A. The targeted behavior by country A may or may not change. But it's pretty certain that US wheat prices will crash, and you know the rest of that story better than I."

"Man oh man, seems like there should be a better way," commented Jack.

"You just said a mouthful," responded Salt, "but keep in mind that in early 2020, the United States and China signed a trade deal that in theory was supposed to fix some of this as between the United States and China. But then along came the COVID-19 pandemic, which the United States blamed on China. That complicated an already very messy state of affairs. Frankly, it was hard to assess whether the trade deal with China was on or off. Only time will tell what, if anything, comes of that in whatever is the new normal." As he was speaking, Salt was thinking to himself how right Jack was and about the provocative discussions at Margie's dinner party. Maybe there was no escaping this stuff.

CHAPTER TWELVE

Louise and Salt Talk Turkey

The next day was Thursday, and the doorbell rang at precisely 1:01 p.m. It was Louise, dressed again in a black pantsuit, smiling, and clearly ready to get going. She wasn't wearing a mask but took a socially distant seat at the kitchen table and declined his offer of a mask. Salt also offered coffee; she preferred water. Salt asked if well water would do. She responded, "Do you have any bottled water?"

Salt responded truthfully, "Sorry, but I have never bought a bottle of water." She took a glass of the well water, not asking if it had been run though a filter. Salt concluded this was going to be a long afternoon. No sense injecting more irritation than necessary.

Louise started out with her remaining litany of questions. That took the first hour and a half. Salt wasn't good with names and had to agree to come up with information for a long list of non-US citizens he had come into contact with over the years as well as US citizens who could attest to his straight arrowness. Salt must have passed that part of the test, because she did not up and leave in the middle. In reality, Salt was a pretty plain vanilla guy.

After producing another glass of well water, Salt decided it was time to set the stage for more serious talk. "Now that we've gone through all of that, what is this really about? You're not dumb, but you're playing dumb. You're not that good at acting. You've been around—in the Agency and other related organizations—for a long time, so you're a survivor in tough environments. You're not likely to want to babysit a retiree. Tell me who you really are and what Stuart really wants from me."

"Fair questions," she responded. "I'll go against all of my training and trust you and your discretion. You seem to have some, and that's more than you can say about many men. I've done many things, including being a CIA field agent. I have been loaned to Stuart for this project. I grew up in the United States and France, did undergraduate work at the Sorbonne in Paris, was recruited after that by the CIA in part because of my language skills. My real name is not Louise but Marie Louise, but the Agency thinks that sounds too French, so I'm Louise. I have gone through the full range of training with the Agency, including the martial arts and firearms. I'm a very good shot. I've served in Asia but more in Europe, especially Eastern Europe. I have used firearms in the field. There have been fatalities but no innocent victims. Those who have passed got what they deserved. I'm not a female Jason Bourne, but I'm good at what I do. But I want to do more, something more subtle than my prior assignments. I would like to be attached to the diplomatic corps in a significant role, but most of those roles seem to go to white males. I am not a male and I have mixed racial origins. I need a mentor and some experience that counts. Nobody in their right mind would think that attaching myself to you and this role that Stuart is making up as he goes makes sense. But I think you may have more to you than meets the eye. I'm willing to experiment and invest some time and effort around this."

"Okay," said Salt as he took a deep breath and tried to take all of that in. "You win the contest for candor, but several more questions. First, what do you mean by being attached to me? I don't need either a helper or a bodyguard."

"Wrong," she said. "That's what I thought at first, but if Stuart's hairbrained scheme works at all, you'll be subject to some level of risk. We'll get back to what Stuart wants, but if you're successful in calming some of the global diplomatic disarray, you will be viewed as an inconvenient and dangerous person by those who benefit from disarray—and there are plenty of those, both in the United States and outside. Perhaps it's assuming the worst, but you do need someone to watch your back."

Salt came to life. "Whoa," he said. "I would never create or buy into that much danger. You can't make this stuff up."

"I'm not making this up," she responded. "If you're even modestly successful, you'll be upsetting the efforts of people like the Russians, the Iranians, and the North Koreans. Russia has arranged for former spies to be poisoned in the UK. You must know the stories of the 2006 poisoning murder of Litvinenko and then the attempts a decade or so later on two others, Sergei Skripal and his daughter. God only knows what the Iranians have done through ISIS and otherwise, and North Korea's supreme leader hired women to knock off family members in the Singapore airport. The good news is that you don't think you're good enough to pull this off, and if you're right, you have nothing to worry about."

Salt thought for a moment, rubbing his chin to get rid of nervous energy. "Even if you're right, you don't seem like the type who would want to follow me around as a bag carrier."

"Now you hold on," she nearly yelled. "I'm no damned bag carrier. I'm a woman, and that makes me seem less dangerous to some, which is a tactical advantage. But I'm fully capable of being equally vigilant eyes and ears in sensitive meetings, and you will need that. So get over it, and be glad I'm willing to humor you and play act as a second fiddle. You may be the conductor, but I'll be the concertmaster—and a good one."

Scrambling to get out of this mess, Salt countered, "You've seen my file. I need to see yours."

"No objection here," she said.

"I'm not suggesting for a minute that any of this makes sense," said Salt. "But assuming it did, this would involve a lot of travel, presumably together. In this *me too* era, how does an old white guy like me feel safe from being accused of harassment or something like that?"

She laughed. "You really are a dinosaur. The chances of you being able to force me to do anything I didn't want to do is zero. Less than zero. You might end up in a bed, but it would be in a hospital. Relax."

Salt felt the blushing take over his face.

"Feels like that's a good place to stop for today," Salt suggested.

"Not yet," she said. "I'm under orders not to come back without understanding where your head is on all of this, even if it is up your ass. That's a direct quote from Stuart."

"Very diplomatic," Salt commented. "First you tell me you can whup my ass, and now you say my head may be up my ass. I feel like I'm having a nuclear hemorrhoid attack. Are you always this gentle? Are you sure you want to be a diplomat when you grow up?"

"Sorry," she said. "I thought you could handle someone being direct."

"I'll get over it," Salt countered. "You leveled with me earlier, so—also against my better judgment—I'll level with you. I'm very confused about what I want to do with my life postretirement, postmarriage, post–everything I cared about. I doubt anyone can pull off what Stuart has in mind—whatever that is. But I've been surprised by recent discussions about how much our diplomatic yo-yo game has messed things up for a lot of ordinary people in ordinary places. If there's a 2 percent shot at helping, it might be worthwhile to try."

"If you want to do this, you need to decide fast; there are other candidates, though you're the preferred party at this point. Moreover, you're the only candidate I'm attached to, so I'm in your corner. What else do you need?"

"The next step," Salt responded, "is for you to get me permission to fly to Canada on my nickel to meet with Rene Marchand, known as Ray in the United States and Toronto, and talk to him about this. Ray is a lawyer with a big Canadian law firm, has a lot of diplomatic experience, and is a good friend from the days when he was involved in the Canadian foreign ministry and UN delegation and I was with State. I trust him and respect his judgment. I want to see what he thinks about the world in general, US-Canadian relations, Europe, and this nutty idea of Stuart's. The mission impossible element of this is to get permission for me to spill the beans to Ray. To be clear, I'm not saying I'll do anything, but I am thinking about it. If Stuart says no, that's fine and understandable, and then my answer will be no thanks. By the way, I want to use that encrypted shoe phone you gave me to get hold of Ray. And no, you're not invited to this meeting. Again, to be clear, I'm paying my own way up there if we can get the meeting cleared for me. No strings attached."

"Fair enough, I guess," she hissed. "I'll be back to you tomorrow or Saturday." Noticing that the afternoon was gone, she said, "I need to head back to DC but would like something to eat first. Have any suggestions?"

"I could also use a bite to eat," said Salt, "but there's still nothing in this house. Follow me into town, and we'll have a quick bite downtown at the local diner."

As Salt and Louise were waiting for their meal at Helen's, Margie walked in with a female friend. Salt thought about the line from *Casablanca* in which Bogart says something like "Of all of the gin joints in the world, she had to pick this one." He introduced Louise as a colleague and was surprised that he was blushing again. Louise noticed.

CHAPTER THIRTEEN

Canadian Reality Check

Louise passed her first test with flying colors by getting the Canadian junket approved, so Salt called to arrange to meet with Ray Marchand in Canada. Ray split his time between his law firm's offices in Montreal and Toronto. Salt asked him for two to three hours in either city for a highly confidential matter that would not result in any revenue for his law firm. True to form, Ray said he could clear Monday afternoon in Toronto.

Early Monday morning, Salt drove in to Dulles Airport, boarded a small regional jet that was operating despite the coronavirus and recession, landed in Toronto, went through customs, grabbed a cab and noticed that the driver was wearing a mask, put on his own, and then experienced the traffic hell that was the Gardiner Expressway from the airport to downtown Toronto. He was glad he had scheduled plenty of time for transit. After grabbing a cold-cut sandwich at a shop in Ray's building and putting on his mask again, he took an elevator up to the forty-third floor and waited. Suddenly, this seemed like a nutty idea again. How was he going to explain this in a rational way? And who would believe the idea had a prayer of success? Thank goodness he had picked an old friend to try this out on.

Ray walked into the office reception area and greeted him with a booming voice, even through his mask, clearly glad to see Salt. "I have been wanting to see you and share stories about US politics. What's up?"

"Nothing we can discuss in your reception area," cautioned Salt. They headed for a small conference room.

After they were ensconced in a small but comfortable conference room with a great view and each had a cup of coffee, Salt and Ray exchanged pleasantries and generally caught up. Salt asked about Canadians' view of their young prime minister following Canada's recent failure to gain a seat on the UN Security Council (losing to Norway and Ireland), whether he would prevail in the next election and what that meant for US-Canada relations, and how Canadians were reacting to the early days of the USMCA treaty that replaced NAFTA.

As they were completing their catch-up, Ray said, "Salt, before we get into the details of whatever is on your agenda, I need to ask you about a couple of things. First up is the Black Lives Matter movement and what is going on in your country. The use of the military to clear Lafayette Park during the George Floyd disturbances last summer was scary—it looked more like Russia than across the street from the White House. Ugly. Many of us can't understand how the US got here. We in Canada feel a little like the younger sibling of an older brother who has been convicted of a serious crime. We don't understand, and we're lost without that older brother."

"Well," said Salt, "as an old white guy who likely has a few racist bones in his body, I am not the most qualified to speak to that topic, but it needs to be recognized and dealt with as the shameful situation it is. We have to do better in all kinds of ways. Dealing with police profiling and brutality is just a starting point—and a relatively easy one. We haven't yet gone far enough there. These issues, combined with our urgent infrastructure deficiencies, may mean that we need what amounts to a Marshall Plan for America.

"I've not tried to explain it like this before, but consider two museums in Washington, the Holocaust Museum and the National Museum of African American History and Culture. Both are evidence of shameful racial treatment with major impacts on the world. These things make you wonder, how in the world did that happen? If you go to the African American museum, it takes you through the experience of blacks over four hundred years in what is now the US. History teaches us that, to a significant extent, the United States was built on the backs of blacks. But because of our history, there has not been fair sharing of the opportunities that represent the fruits of that labor.

"You know, there have been many outstanding and recognized accomplishments by blacks in the US, but the thing is, they have to overcome not only competition but a terrible history of bias that creates barriers of all kinds. There is systematic racial bias in the US. Period. We all need to understand that. This will likely never be fully remedied, but the Black Lives Matter movement, with its rainbow of supporters, may just force more fairness. The movement needs to be broad, determined, and successful. This is important. Its time has come, and in the long run the protestors are actually doing the United States a great service."

After a few moments of silence, Ray responded. "Thanks. Maybe that is a useful way to start thinking about it. Let's switch gears and move on to the second matter. How in God's name did the US flub so badly the response to COVID-19? We are sitting here in January 2021, essentially a year after the pandemic began, and the US is still fighting what amounts to a third or fourth wave of the disease without ever really getting your arms around it while second and third tier countries have done better. You guys have the best epidemiologists in the world and have thrown billions at it without getting it under control. And you have a massive recession and job loss to boot. How did that happen? We all hope that one or more of these vaccines will do the trick, but only time will tell I gather."

Salt responded quickly. "One word: leadership. Maybe a few others, like divisive politics and lack of popular will to make sacrifices for the greater good for longer than a couple of months without good leadership."

"Well," said Ray, "I gather you are not here to talk about either of those topics, but as a friend and in the interest of candor, I need to say that the racial issues in the United States and its mishandling of the COVID-19 crisis detract significantly from its ability to regain its leadership role in the world. The United States is diminished by this history you describe and the related current events. People just shake their heads."

"Well," said Salt, "we've already agreed on something. Now we need to turn to other aspects of US politics, which is what I'm here to talk about, but with important ground rules. Ray, I hate to do this, but I need to say up front that if you cannot agree to the ground rules, I'll fully understand, and we can cut this way short."

"Okay, friend, lay them on me," Ray responded.

Salt began, talking slowly. "The ground rules are first that this meeting never happened and you won't write it up; second, you never discussed the subject matter of this meeting before it became public, if it ever does; and third, you can't share the content of the meeting with the Canadian government, where I know you have lots of good and reliable friends, unless I clear it. You and Canada would get a head start but not an exclusive. In return, I will follow the same rules, except that I can share the content of this meeting on a confidential basis with Stuart Bacon, who knows I'm here, a colleague from the CIA I would be working with, and President Evans."

"Hmm," murmured Ray. "Well, you have certainly piqued my curiosity. Since you're saying it's your way or the highway, I guess I have no choice, but this better be good. In order to have some balance here, I need to be able to discuss whatever this is on a confidential basis with our foreign minister. Nothing in writing."

"Thanks, Ray," responded Salt, who without thinking held out his hand to shake and then quickly pulled it back. Both smiled about the gesture. Salt then started talking through the barebones outline that Stuart Bacon had shared with him. After getting through that, Salt said, "So there are two basic questions for you, Ray. What is your assessment of the diplomatic status, influence, and credibility of the United States, and does this hairbrained scheme have a chance to make things better?"

"Well," said Ray slowly, "there are a lot of layers to this. So I'm going to do what you Americans only sometimes do when you say you are going to tell it like it is. I'll actually do that."

"First, America is viewed as somewhat racist and xenophobic. We've already talked about race, and the xenophobic nature of your immigration policies have the Statue of Liberty weeping under her mask. Enough said.

"Second, there is the trust factor. Nobody, and I mean nobody, trusts the United States anymore. We don't trust your word, your actions, your motives, your politics, your people, or your follow-through. Assume President Evans is sort of like what the president seems: a decent, if naïve, middle-of-the-roader. One decent administration is not enough to undo the doubt. Trust dissolves a lot faster than it forms. If the president is trustworthy, can the president be reelected? Who and what follows? Because your politics are so screwed up and divided, nobody knows. The divided politics give rise to a divided government in both the administration and Congress. And there are lots of showboating and promises that could not be kept even if the promise maker wanted to.

"Third, nobody knows who is left. The diplomatic corps seems a shadow of its former self. Clearly, there remain some very good and loyal people—and they are very good—but not enough. In some areas, the diplomatic infrastructure needs to be rebuilt almost from scratch. No offense, but it speaks volumes that Stuart has decided to bring you, who amounts to an outsider, in from the cold to start fixing some things. And then there is the fact that nobody is comfortable with their current read of the situation—or how stable it is. The last administration seemed to clean house every so often in order to eliminate dissent. What will things look like in a year?"

Ray took a breath and continued: "Think about all the things the United States has backed out of, threatened, or criticized: the Paris Climate Accord; the Trans-Pacific Partnership; NATO; the Iranian nuclear treaty; the World Health Organization; the World Trade Organization; negotiations with Russia on the New START nuclear arms reduction treaty; even UNESCO for heaven's sake. Nothing is safe. Real countries don't do this sort of thing. It is one thing to

INHERITANCE OF CRISES AND DYSFUNCTION ★ 63

say some things are out of whack and need to be fixed. It is another to tweet insults on a regular basis and abandon treaties by tweet. Unbelievable. Wasn't it one of your presidents who said, 'Speak softly but carry a big stick'? That seems to be a lost art.

"Those of us outside the United States will be in a show-me mode—prove that leadership is different, that there is followership in the electorate and Congress, new blood in the diplomatic corps, stability, and credibility.

"Think of it this way. After 9/11, the rest of the world closed ranks with the United States, including expending blood and treasure on some things that didn't turn out very well. If 9/11 happened today, we would maybe send thoughts and prayers but not troops, equipment, or money."

Ray continued along the same lines for an hour or more, including details as to issues in which Canada had a particular interest, with Salt interrupting only occasionally with a question or carefully worded objection. Salt had been taught by his father not to try to argue with an angry person, and Ray was using the occasion to unload on Salt.

"Well, I asked for it," acknowledged Salt. "And you gave it to me, though I noticed that you did not complain about the lack of follow-through by the United States on buying Greenland. Recognizing the depth of the problem is only step one. How do we start to fix it?"

Ray thought for a few minutes. "As I said earlier, there is no shortcut available here. You can get started, but there will be no miracles. Start by undoing as much unnecessary damage as you can. It is helpful that NAFTA was redone as the US-Mexico-Canada trade agreement, or USMCA, with some beneficial changes. Beg your way back into the Trans-Pacific Partnership treaty and the Paris climate accord. Make your devotion to NATO clear. And by the way, that does not mean you need to buy your way into a better place; other countries should pay their fair share. Think creatively about Iran, though that one may not be recoverable. Stop making things worse in Jerusalem. And, yes, leaving Greenland alone is okay.

"Then show the world you're serious about rebuilding your team and your image by naming to key ambassadorships solid members of the diplomatic corps or other serious people. Break the habit of trying to make big donors into ambassadors. You can't afford not to do that right now, even though big donors seemed to no longer be safe from removal under President Pope.

"Jettison all Twitter accounts. Period.

"Get your act together on US immigration. This is very hard, I know, but in recent years, this has created a very big stain on the US image, which it can ill afford these days.

"Get used to the idea that on the economy, climate change, terrorism, cybersecurity, and so many other things, the United States is no longer independent but rather interdependent. A first among nearer and nearer equals, if you will. The United States is no longer a private island. You can't accomplish very much unilaterally anymore.

"Before you get on a plane to be the roving secret diplomatic fixer, make sure you know how far President Evans will go along these lines. The worst thing for you would be to overpromise and underdeliver to the countries you'll be meeting with. The only thing you have going for you is that not many remember you, and those who do still think of you as a straight shooter. Don't lose that. Get the president to give you comfort on these issues.

"And by the way, my friend, you may as well make it clear that you're not willing to do this forever, because that's how long it will take.

"So, will it work? Not in the short term. It might help over the long term if you're not double-crossed. It will not undo the last four years—that will take a long time. It would be a start, might help and can't hurt."

At the end of an intense discussion that eventually became more two-sided, Salt thanked Ray and said, "This is why I needed to talk to you. I appreciate it."

"What else can I do for you?" asked Ray.

Salt hesitated for a moment and then said, "There is one other thing I want to ask about. What is Canada's view of the World Health Organization these days?"

"My God," said Ray. "Why do you ask about that? It is important, but you already have a long list of highly visible diplomatic issues to think about. Even with the COVID-19 still hanging over us, I would not get tangled up with the WHO controversies as a priority."

"I appreciate that," responded Salt quietly. "It's a personal matter. My wife, Meredith, was a nurse and contracted the virus during the pandemic. If I take on this other stuff, I owe it to her to see if the world's health threat response systems can be improved."

Ray responded carefully. "I don't know enough to comment, but I'll make some quiet calls. The WHO didn't cover itself with glory on COVID-19, but I don't know whether that was China, the WHO, the Pope administration, or all of them screwing things up."

"Thanks, Ray," said Salt quietly. They finished with a much more normal conversation and best wishes.

Salt had a lot to think about on his way home. The last thing he needed was more aggravation, but the Gardiner Expressway to the airport during rush hour reminded him of Washington traffic. And to make things worse, he forgot that he would be going through US customs in the Toronto airport, not at his destination, and he had to run to avoid missing the flight. He sat quietly during the short flight, trying to digest what he had heard from Ray and thinking about next steps. Shortly after landing in the early evening, he decided to stay overnight in Tysons, Virginia, near Langley. He would call Louise and try to get together somewhere quiet where he could debrief her and get her reaction. He needed to talk to someone, and right now, she was the only person on the face of the earth he could talk to about this.

CHAPTER FOURTEEN

Napkin Principles

They got together in a quiet corner of a restaurant in McLean where the graying evening crowd was thinning out. Quiet was easy to find, and they were able to sit at a social distance and avoid the use of masks after they were seated. Salt was dead tired but needed something to eat and to relax in addition to having someone to talk with. Louise arrived a few minutes after he did and asked for the debrief. Salt started talking, aided by a masked waiter bringing a Manhattan, which Salt sipped, and a large glass of water, which he guzzled.

Salt opened by asking Louise if she had ever seen the movie *Get Smart* and if she understood the meaning of the phrase "cone of silence." She answered in the affirmative. "Good," said Salt, "because we're now in a very secure cone of silence. This does not even go as far as Stuart unless we agree that it should. Agreed?" She did.

Salt opened the discussion by summarizing his chat with Ray. He then said, "Louise, I have to be honest. I don't see how this project is going to work. There are serious issues here than cannot be resolved even during a four-year presidential term. I initially thought this might involve a four-month commitment. It involves way more than that. And I would need high-level support for meetings outside of the United States, commitments to change that could be reliably delivered upon. I'm not sure President Evans and Stuart can deliver. I could end up looking like more of an idiot than I actually am."

Louise was quiet for a few moments. She looked at Salt and realized that he was stressed out and that this gig was on life support. She tried to be comforting. "Okay—let's start with what we can control. We can't control the fact that this is going to take a longer and more sustained effort than you thought. That is what it is. To kick off the effort, you need more detail about the Evans doctrine—or whatever you want to call the president's foreign policy—than you now know and, if there is enough coincidence of thought, extract some promises. Let's think about what you need."

Louise grabbed a dry cocktail napkin from an adjoining table, pulled out a pen, and wrote "Necessary Principles" across the top. The waiter came by, and they ordered another round of drinks and some appetizers. They then got to work on the napkin.

They started broadly with Salt pontificating about what was needed and Louise understanding that he needed to vent. As the discussion continued, she pushed back more often and with more force. In the end, they decided to limit Salt's Necessary Principles to ten, then eleven, and then twelve. It was not easy.

This is what the first iteration of the list looked like:

Necessary Principles

1. Stuart Bacon is secretary of state or director of national intelligence.
2. Pepper reports directly to Bacon and President Evans, including reasonable direct access to Evans.
3. Professional diplomats as ambassadors in places like Canada, UK, France, Germany, Russia, China, Australia, India, Turkey, Japan, Israel, and Mexico.
4. Good faith attempts to rejoin Paris Climate Accord.
5. Good faith attempts to rejoin Trans-Pacific Partnership (TPP) treaty.
6. Much more limited use of tariffs.

7. Unconditional support of NATO.
8. Arms control discussions with Russia.
9. New and different approach to North Korea, coordinated with South Korea and Japan.
10. Reopen good faith discussions with Iran and parties to the nuclear treaty (Joint Comprehensive Plan of Action).
11. Commitment to restore professional senior staffing at State Department.
12. Fix Ukraine.

"Well," said Louise, "that is a napkin full for sure. And the assessment of the president being able to deliver on all the items is *no fucking way*. But some of this is easy. Take the State Department staffing, for example. Not an issue. But the ambassadorships, on the other hand, are a different story. You know that many of these—not all—have already been promised to big donors. Hard to imagine President Evans picking up the phone to call a big donor—call him Jack—who has been promised London and saying, 'Jack, I've got good news and bad news. We have a guy you've never heard of who is about to waste two years of his life on a diplomatic mission impossible. We need to humor him, and he says he won't take on the mission unless we put a professional staffer in charge of the embassy in London. As a result, you don't have to move to London and meet the queen and all of that. But we have some pretty exciting opportunities that you can pick from. And if you help us reduce the campaign debt, there is always Norway or the Caribbean.' The president is going to say, 'Salt, you don't know my donor Jack, and you don't know jack shit about the realities of this stuff.' And that will be the end of this exercise."

"Sounds like a good result to me." Salt nodded.

Louise responded, "Just for the hell of it, let's call the napkin we have been using Napkin A. We will start a new napkin and call it Napkin B. Let's see where the give might be. They started through the list and discussed each point, item by item.

Somewhat to Salt's surprise, Louise took the lead this time through. Maybe it was the alcohol.

"Stuart needs to be secretary of state," she stated. "Director of national intelligence is just too limiting. You need Stuart to help move the State Department bureaucracy, or what's left of it, when need be. And you need to be able to get into the Oval Office when need be, so number two is okay as is. As we discussed, item three, the ambassador thing, is a nonstarter."

"But that could be a strong early signal to the key countries, and it's easy to do from a logistics standpoint," protested Salt. "It would likely find bipartisan support on the Hill."

"Get over it," Louise shot back. "Think of something else."

Salt took another sip of his Manhattan and thought for a few minutes. "Let's require that, in the G-7 and selected other countries, there be a senior person acceptable to me that is read into the project and reports directly to Stuart and not the ambassador. This project will be out of bounds for political appointees."

"Worth a try," Louise responded. "Items four, five, six, and eleven should be acceptable as they are. Items four, five, and six were part of Evans's platform, and Stuart will insist on item eleven. How about item seven and NATO?"

"Well," said Salt, "unconditional is a strong word, I guess. How about if we say, 'strong support of NATO that does not assume we stop pushing them to pay for committed defense costs,' or something along those lines?"

"Okay," responded Louise. "And arms control negotiations with Russia and fixing Ukraine?"

"Important but outside the scope of this," acknowledged Salt.

"Done," she said. "Now, for the easy ones, North Korea and Iran."

"I don't know," said Salt. "I'm too tired and have had too much to drink to take those on. There are no answers. Just say approach to those countries to be closely coordinated with allies. That's all that can be said, in reality, but those issues will be front and center in discussions with many countries, especially those who have supported aggressive sanctions. But we need to put on the list the New START talks with Russia."

"Okay, let's look at Napkin B now," Louise suggested. And they did.

Necessary Principles—Napkin B

1. Stuart Bacon is secretary of state.
2. Pepper reports directly to Bacon and President Evans, including reasonable direct access to Evans.
3. In G-7 and other selected countries, a direct contact in the embassy, acceptable to Pepper, will be established with such contacts reporting to Pepper and the secretary of state with respect to this project; project not to be shared with political appointees.
4. Good faith attempts to rejoin Paris Climate Accord.
5. Good faith attempts to rejoin TPP.
6. Much more limited and targeted use of tariffs.
7. Strong support of NATO, not to foreclose pressure on member state defense spending.
8. Approach to North Korea to be closely coordinated with allies, especially South Korea and Japan.
9. Approach to Iran to be closely coordinated with allies and parties to the Iran nuclear treaty (Joint Comprehensive Plan of Action) that the United States withdrew from, and stay out of wars in the Middle East.
10. Commitment to strengthen professional senior staffing at State Department.
11. Meaningful and rational comprehensive immigration reform.
12. Rapid movement toward renewed New START talks without requiring China to participate.

"Okay for now," said Salt, "but I need to sleep on this. I'll call you in the morning. Sorry to ask you to do this, but I don't have a computer with me. Can you get this typed and cleaned up a bit. I doubt the president will be impressed with a napkin. The real question now is, assuming I'm still willing to try do something, what is my next step? Meet with Stuart?"

"No," Louise blurted out. "We—not just you—need to meet with the president and Stuart ASAP and in person. You need to unload on them with the input from Ray in Toronto, show them the Napkin B list, and watch how they react. And if this is going to get launched at all, that needs to happen sooner rather than later, that's for sure. Now, get some rest and call me in the morning."

As they were walking out of the restaurant, Salt asked to be reminded where the nearest Marriott was, and as they said good night, Salt added, "By the way, do me a favor and don't throw those napkins away. I may want to frame them someday—or shred them."

CHAPTER FIFTEEN

Napkin Negotiations

The next morning, Salt called Louise on what he now called the "shoe phone" and said he was willing to meet with the president and Stuart and gauge their response to his report on Canada and Napkin B. He asked if Louise could arrange for the meeting. Her answer was a bit frosty. "No, this is a meeting that you need to set up. Let me know what you arrange."

"Sorry," said Salt. "I thought you were insisting on being there."

Louise was doing a slow burn. "I am, but you need to make that happen without me looking like your calendar keeper. This is a test. Don't screw it up."

Salt called Stuart and left a message asking for a prompt meeting with Stuart and the president that Louise would also attend. Stuart called back several hours later in a huff about how the president had a day job that did not involve fitting Salt in when it suited Salt. Salt responded, "Sorry, but I thought this was a priority. Call me when some slots become available. In the meantime, I'll go back to the farm and unpack a few boxes."

"Don't do that until I get back to you," Stuart demanded. "You know, it's going to be hard to make this work if you live two and a half hours away."

"Yep, life's a bitch, but it's my life. And most of these countries you want me to talk with are not in our time zone anyhow." Salt hung up and decided to take a walk around the nearby Tysons mall, which he had not been to for years, while waiting for Stuart to call back. He was surprised at how empty the mall was—of both people and stores. The COVID-19 pandemic and the recession had clearly taken a toll. There were lots of For Lease signs.

Salt wasn't sure, but based on the few store windows he looked at, it seemed remotely possible that his wardrobe was out of date. But he had several suits that had been made in Hong Kong, and he decided he'd be damned if he would get rid of those.

Stuart called back in a few hours. They were on with the president at nine o'clock the next morning. Stuart advised him to stay put in the hotel in McLean, and as long as he was around, Stuart said they should get together at a private club in DC that evening so they could prepare. "I'll have to bring Louise," said Salt.

"Damn right," responded Stuart. It seemed like she was in.

Louise did the driving, and they met with Stuart at 7:30 p.m. in a corner of a sparsely populated dining room. They each ordered lightly and started on a bottle of pinot noir. Salt opened with a recounting of his meeting in Toronto with Ray. Stuart did not seem to be surprised, acknowledging that he had been given similar, if less pointed, lectures by diplomats from other countries. But Salt's version from Canada was another wake-up call. Stuart was in sales mode.

"Hell, if we thought it was easy, we wouldn't have asked you," commented Stuart.

"And if I thought it was easy, I wouldn't be laying these take-it-leave-it demands on you," said Salt quietly.

Stuart came to life. "Whoa. What demands?"

"Look, Stuart," said Salt, "before you get in a huff, look at this from my standpoint and that of other countries. I just can't get myself in a situation where I represent the US position on issue X to be solution A when solution A is a nonstarter in the United States. I'm a dead duck if that happens. And beyond that, I need to know the US position on key issues before I decide whether to even try doing some good here. I need to cover my ass in advance. And the same concerns apply to Louise."

"Just show me the damn list," responded Stuart.

Louise handed him the typed version of Napkin B. Stuart started to read and began to twitch.

Stuart looked at Louise. "Louise, do you buy into this list, or is this Salt pouring salt into open wounds—no pun intended?"

"I'm in," she said.

"I was afraid of that. Look, I could bitch and moan about this, but that would not be productive. You guys have got to look at this at two levels. Frankly, the president probably agrees with most of this. And so at one level, the president and I can have your backs. But there is a second level that's a reality. The president can't act—or appear to act—unilaterally on a number of these issues. There is the State Department buy-in—thanks for your vote for me as secretary, by the way—but I'm pretty sure you don't get a vote. And then there is the dysfunctional Congress. We can talk to the president about what the president's policy will be, and I will tell you what I think, but we can't have you blabbing about the president's position on this stuff before there is a public position. The president's ass also needs to be covered, for Christ's sake."

They then walked through the list item by item and discussed the issues and nuances and practical problems. It became clear that important factors for all at the table and the president would include (1) who Salt and Louise would be relating to, (2) whether those persons had loose lips, and (3) how strongly Salt and Louise would articulate the president's position on various issues.

As they were wrapping up, Stuart simply said, "Thanks. I'll meet with the president at nine, and we'll see you at 9:15. The most we will have will be until 9:45."

Louise dropped Salt off at the Tysons Marriott. There wasn't much to be said. Besides, Salt was not in the mood to give her an opportunity to comment on his wardrobe. Down deep, he knew what she thought.

CHAPTER SIXTEEN

White House Input

Salt picked up Louise in the morning, and they arrived at the White House at nine o'clock. After having their temperatures taken, waiting for fifteen minutes, and putting on their masks, they were shown into the Oval Office. That office, in and of itself, was intimidating. It was apparent that President Evans was not done moving in, but that did not detract from the awe factor. The Oval Office was the Oval Office, after all, and it looked pretty much like it did on TV. Salt wondered to himself how the hell he had gotten there.

Stuart was there, and the president was jovial and welcoming. Maybe the president was a morning person. They exchanged pleasantries, but the president was not into much small talk today. "Let's cut to the chase, folks. I appreciate your going to talk to your buddy in Canada, Salt, and the thoughts outlined on your Plan B paper. And I understand why you need me to cover your backsides—otherwise we will blow your credibility, which is what you bring to the party, Salt. So, look, three things. First, I would be crazy to do something that would destroy the mission. Second, I have looked at your paper and generally agree with what is outlined there. I think we need to drop the immigration bullet for now, because nobody knows yet what comprehensive immigration reform is—so it's meaningless. Third, I can't go public with positions on these other issues now.

That's just a political reality. You folks are rightly focused on things international. I get it. But only US citizens vote in our elections, and we have a ton of domestic issues that just landed in our laps, including COVID-19, the recession, the deficit, and Black Lives Matter. Reminds me of the old Johnny Cash song, 'fifteen tons and what do you get, another day older and deeper in debt.' We don't any longer say, 'America first,' but the reality is that domestic issues, like health care, finishing the recession recovery, and the Black Lives Matter movement, need to come first. Look, you can honestly represent my position to be consistent with your outline, but if someone leaks it, I may have to deny it. Plausible deniability. Yep," the president said, staring at Salt and sighing, "we don't have to like it, but we're here for the greater good. That means we really have to be very careful about who you talk with and what you say to whom.

"That's it," the president concluded. "I need to know by noon tomorrow whether you're willing to undertake this mission. If not, no harm done. If yes, we need to get a move on. By the way, I got the line about direct access to me. That's okay, but the reality is that Stuart and I are of the same mind on this. Your first port of call should be Stuart, but if you need to talk to me, we'll get you in as we did today. Besides, I'll want regular updates. Have a good one."

It was apparent that they were being dismissed. But Salt wasn't done.

"There is one other thing, President Evans," Salt injected.

"What's that?" the president asked.

Salt looked out the window so his face was not visible to the others and said, "I need to add one more item the Plan B agenda."

Stuart and Louise gulped. The president looked quizzical.

With damp eyes, Salt turned to the president. "My wife, Meredith, died last year of the coronavirus while working as a nurse in a major hospital in Northern Virginia. She had been a nurse for many years but had managed several years ago to get into a doctors' office so she could have more regular hours. When the pandemic arrived with force in this area, she volunteered to work in the emergency room of a major hospital, she contracted the virus, and it killed her. If I'm going to take on this assignment, I owe it to her to look into how we address global health threats, including whether the World Health Organization needs attention. I'm sorry, but that needs to be part of the package. Please be assured that I have no interest in being part of a blame game on this."

The room fell silent. After a few moments, the president responded. "Two things. I'm very sorry about your wife. But words like that are meaningless really. I get that. If you want to explore the world health morass, okay, and we will provide some staff and other support. But it cannot get in the way of the rest of the agenda. We are not going to let the WHO fall apart any time soon."

The president stood up and saluted. Shaking hands was out. There was clearly nothing more to be said, and Salt and Louise left. Stuart followed in a few seconds.

"That went as well as it could have gone until the end," Stuart remarked. "I wish you would have given me a heads-up about that, Salt."

"Sorry, Stuart," Salt responded. "It came as a bit of a surprise to me, to tell you the truth. You have a right to be pissed."

Stuart paused for a moment, taking in Salt's response, and then said, "It would be great if you could decide today what you're going to do. If that happened, we would try to set up briefings for you starting tomorrow afternoon. We would like to have this kicked off with meetings—probably in the UK—next week. And Salt, I really am very sorry. I didn't know how Meredith died."

Salt and Louise left, climbed into Salt's dirty ten-year-old Volvo, and crossed the bridge into Virginia. What they needed was a quiet coffee shop with glazed doughnuts and chocolate croissants. They found one, got what was needed for their caffeine and sugar fixes, and sat down in a socially distanced area.

Louise broke the silence. "Well, we got most of what we asked for."

"Sorry for the surprise, Louise, but my new ask was actually pretty spontaneous," explained Salt. "After it came to me, it became important." Salt paused and then changed the topic. "I'll say one thing, neither of us has even been, or ever again will be, in a meeting anything like that. Holy shit!"

"So, what do we do?" she asked.

"I guess I don't have the courage to say no," Salt admitted. "If I say no, I see myself getting up in the morning every day, looking in the mirror, and thinking what a chicken shit I was for saying no. But that doesn't mean you need to have the same hang-ups. Where's your head?"

Louise paused for a few moments. "You're right. And even though I don't care for playing second fiddle in this ensemble, I'm in. And playing second fiddle means I have plausible deniability like the president."

Salt grinned a bit. "This reminds me of when I played basketball in high school. I sat on the end of the bench unless they needed someone to go in and take a beating in a game we were losing by a mile. It was hopeless."

Louise said, "But despite the odds, you went into the game and didn't quit."

"Right," acknowledged Salt.

"So," said Louise, "tell me more about this world health element of the program."

Salt looked puzzled. "Well, to be honest, I don't know. I haven't really thought it out. We need to get a lot more homework done on this, and you can take a pass on that element of the program. You didn't sign up for this on either of the napkins."

Louise leaned forward and asked, with some wonderment, "Are you thinking of taking on the World Health Organization and the United Nations? Maybe your real name is Don Quixote."

Salt responded, "The World Health Organization is essentially the United Nations. If a country belongs to the United Nations, it can be a member of the WHO. There are nearly two hundred members. At the risk of oversimplifying things, the WHO is supposed to stop or at least arrest things like the coronavirus. That didn't happen in connection with COVID-19. I have a feeling that, like our government, the WHO could have done better, but my guess is that the WHO is essential, and most of the fault lies elsewhere. But I have no interest in a backward-looking investigation and trying to assign blame. That wouldn't make

Meredith rest easier. The history is of interest to me only to the extent it illuminates what needs to be done to fix things. I'm interested in speed and effectiveness. It no doubt makes sense to have something like the WHO, but maybe we need to have something more. Perhaps a combination of the Epidemic Intelligence Service of the Centers for Disease Control and Prevention and small dream teams of experts able to act as pandemic special forces units and go into consenting countries, do the necessary, and ask later for forgiveness rather than waiting for permission. Maybe this already exists, but I need to know. Anyhow, this needs a lot more thought than I have given it, and there are already multiple investigations ongoing. Two things we know for sure now. Pandemics are not mere historical anomalies, and they are serious stuff."

Louise thought for a few minutes and then said, "Well, it's admirable and probably needed, but I have to get my head around it. In the meantime, we need to jump on phase one if we're going to agree to proceed. I think you need to call Stuart."

Salt called Stuart and gave him the news.

"Great," Stuart said. "Show up at the State Department at noon tomorrow for the beginning of a day and a half of briefings. Bring five passport photos and think about buying a decent suit. They still wear suits overseas. You'll be a consultant to the State Department, and we will negotiate over the next few days a fair per diem compensation and expense deal. You won't become wealthy doing this, but you knew that. Let me talk to Louise."

Salt handed the shoe phone to Louise, who mostly listened and from time to time said, "Uh huh." When the call was over, she handed the phone back and said, "I need to go home and pack and also pick up a bunch of stuff at the Agency, so please take me back to my apartment. You need to go shopping. I'll pick you up at the Marriott at 11:00 a.m. sharp tomorrow."

"Okay, boss," deadpanned Salt, "but I will do my shopping by buying American in Carterville."

Louise shook her head and rolled her eyes.

CHAPTER SEVENTEEN

Global Briefing 101

They arrived on time at noon the next day, Thursday, at the State Department, had their temperatures taken as they entered, were issued masks, and were hustled into a rather lavish conference room with a light lunch and five people waiting for them. None of these folks were household names, and it seemed unlikely that they were political. They were bright and clearly wondered what the hell was going on, but they were also smart enough not to ask. There was the inevitable PowerPoint projector but no briefing books. Stuart joined five minutes later, after the standard introductions had been completed and folks had started on their sandwiches.

Stuart grabbed a sandwich and then convened the meeting, speaking through his mask. "Louise and Salt, we have been joined by a group of senior geographical and subject matter experts to give you a general update on an extremely broad range of topics today and tomorrow. This briefing team has been told that I will likely be nominated to become secretary of state and that the president and I have asked you to engage in some highly confidential meetings overseas that will require you to have a solid level of general knowledge but not be on the cutting edge of policies, which in any event are in the process of being formulated. Your efforts will be in the nature of information collection rather than negotiation or policy promotion. These backgrounder sessions have been scheduled for today and tomorrow based on an assumed departure for the UK on Monday morning. You will note that there are no briefing books here. We intend that you walk out of here without any paper, other than your notes, which we trust will be very limited. Before you leave tomorrow, you'll have special diplomatic passports that, despite the bans prohibiting Americans from traveling into the UK and EU, will get you into those regions, so please give your photos to Eric here."

Salt meekly cleared his throat and said, "Oops. Bad start. But I don't have any passport photos with me."

Stuart sighed. "We expected as much; Eric will fix that problem and get your COVID-19 testing done at one of your breaks. Any questions?" There were none, and Stuart took his leave.

The briefings started with the current state of play in various regions and countries and provided some helpful commentary on people and issues. The afternoon sessions covered Europe in general and the larger countries: the UK, its uncertain politics, and the recently concluded and last-minute post-Brexit trade treaty with the EU; the risk of a post-Brexit breakup of the UK; the European Union, including the stability of the EU, the euro, and European banks; the issues associated with the rise of state aid to enterprises such as airlines; the continuing relevance of the G-7 and G-20; and then Russia, Ukraine, Turkey, Iran, Syria, Yemen, Iraq, and Israel. During these discussions, they also touched on the trend toward fragmentation of the global economy and its uncertain implications, including the risk that the Chinese would try to attack the US dollar's status as the global reserve currency. They broke off at 8:00 p.m. and then started again at 9:00 a.m. the next morning. The geographical focus continued with the rest of the Middle East, Africa, China, North and South Korea, Japan, India, Australia, the Asean countries, South America, Mexico, and Canada.

The subject matter discussions focused on the effects of sanctions and tariffs imposed by and against the United States; the Trans-Pacific Partnership and the effects of US withdrawal; the early demise of the US-China trade treaty; developments in Hong Kong; the early days of the USMCA; the Paris Climate Accord and the effects of US withdrawal; NATO and the effects of perceived US indifference, including the surprise reduction of US troops stationed in Germany in the fall of 2020; recent G-7 and G-20 meetings and the ongoing impact of US insults; the emergence of autocratic governments in places like Hungary, Poland, Turkey, and Cambodia (not to mention Russia and China); and finally the effects of direct access by the leaders of hostile nations to President Pope and the lack of records of what was said and agreed to.

Each of the briefings included a who's who discussion of the key players from the countries involved in the subject. Those individual backgrounders were as lively as they were important.

Salt and Louise asked a number of questions, and Salt learned early on in the discussions that Louise was at least as up to date on things as he was, probably more. Earlier in the week, he had thought of her as being in the way; now he was moving in the direction of being grateful for her involvement.

The briefings took the promised day and a half, going into late Friday afternoon. After the sessions broke up on Friday evening, Eric appeared with envelopes for Salt and Louise.

The envelopes included diplomatic passports—several of them with different names and fake ID materials as well. They each received certificates of successful completion of very recent COVID-19 testing that would be as necessary as a passport. Louise's envelope included papers designed to allow her to carry a concealed pistol in several countries. Salt did not say anything but wondered what that was about. There was a note from Stuart saying that Peter Banks of the British Foreign and Commonwealth Office, who Salt knew from the old days and respected, had blocked his day on the following Tuesday for meetings with Salt and Louise. Finally, there were commercial airline tickets in coach for the 9:00 a.m. Monday flight from Dulles to Heathrow Airport, with a separate note that Stuart would try to get them on government flights in the future. The good news was that, in light of continuing low travel volumes associated with the coronavirus episode, they were not in middle seats. But then nobody was. The package had them staying at a Marriott near the old US embassy in London.

Louise dropped Salt at the Marriott in Virginia so he could pick up his car and minimal baggage. "How long do you think we will be out of the country?" Louise asked.

"Beats me," responded Salt. "There is no return ticket in the envelope, so I guess I'll pack for a week. By the way, do you really plan to pack a pistol?"

"Yes, I always do when in the field," she said. "But don't worry. I'll spend some time on the practice range at the Agency this weekend. See you on Monday morning." Salt's eyebrows went up, but she took off before he could say anything.

CHAPTER EIGHTEEN

Small Town America Issues II

It was late enough when they got back to the Marriott that Salt decided to have a drink and dinner there and stay overnight.

The next morning, he remembered that he owed Margie Hatcher a dinner. He screwed up his courage and called her after breakfast and before getting on the road. "I apologize in advance for this short notice, but I owe you a dinner in return for your inviting me to your dinner party. I know this is very short notice, but I wondered if you had time this evening? I'm headed out of the country on business, and if I don't pay up now, it could be a while."

"That would be fine, if you have time," Margie said. "Despite my crowded social calendar, I just happen to be free."

"Great," said Salt. "Where would you like to go? This only place I know is Helen's Place, which is fine, but there must be somewhere else."

"I can probably get us in for dinner at a nice country inn about eight miles out of town, if that would be okay. The food is good, and it's quiet," she said.

"That works for me," said Salt. "And thanks for being willing to make the reservations. Let me know what time to pick you up."

"Unless you hear from me, pick me up at five thirty for a six o'clock reservation."

"Will do," Salt responded. He was surprised at how pleased he was about this.

As Salt drove back to the farm on Saturday morning, he started thinking about what he needed to do to get ready for the trip. He needed a new suit and a hair trim, and he might need a new country casual shirt for the evening's dinner. Rather than going to the farmhouse, he drove into Carterville and parked near the men's store owned by Roy, who he had met at the barbershop. He walked in and saw Roy, apparently the only human in the store, though it was late Saturday morning.

Salt greeted him, saying, "Hi, Roy. You may not remember me, but we met at the barbershop a while back. I need a suit, and I hope you can help me out. But I need it today. If it needs altering so it fits, can I get that done today?"

"I'm the owner, the salesperson, and the tailor," said Roy, "so that won't be an issue. And on Saturday, I compete with college basketball for customers. I can fit it in if we have something you like. What size do you wear, and what are you looking for?"

Salt responded, "Something very boring like a blue suit with a new white shirt and a tie that's any color but red and is not too long. I'm probably something like a 38 tall or a 40 regular, but it's been a long time since I bought a suit off the rack. Back in the day, when I traveled to Hong Kong, I got some suits made there. But for a variety of reasons, I won't be going back there any time soon."

"Well, let's see, a 40 regular should be about right," said Roy. "You know people are wearing suits less and less, so we don't carry very many, and the ones we do have are mostly plain vanilla, like what you're looking for."

As Roy looked through the racks, Salt asked, "How's business these days? Does the trend toward business casual hurt you?"

"Well," responded Roy, "to be honest, we're hanging on by our fingernails. There are lots of factors. Most recently, the COVID-19 lockdown was a killer—in lots of ways—and we had to let everyone but me and one other fellow go. The recovery has been slow. Millennials don't shop in stores like this in a small town and want all casual stuff. For that matter, they don't shop in stores. They shop on the internet, and sometimes they rent their clothes rather than paying for them. Beats the hell out of me. When they do go to a store, they go first to Target or Walmart, and after that to what's left of Macy's or something similar in a mall where there are other things to do. Guys your age come in here, but they're mostly retired and not spending much on new clothes, or are still working and are afraid they will lose their factory job to a cheap immigrant or as a result of the recession. Or they're farmers who don't have money for clothes but would trade me several bushels of grain for a new shirt. Anyhow, all they buy is overalls. And then there's pricing. I sell mostly stuff that's made in the good old USA. These other places get their stuff from China, Bangladesh, southeast Asia, Mexico, you name it. The price competition is fierce, and you sure as hell can't make it up in volume.

"But enough about that—I think you have three choices: a plain navy blue suit or a couple of pinstripes. Want to try one on?"

"Let's start with the blue one," said Salt. It would work with some tricky alterations to shorten the sleeves and take in the chest. Roy helped him find a white shirt and a conservative not-red and not-too-long tie. Roy asked Salt to put on the new suit in the back room. Then Roy put his mask back on and started marking up the suit for the alterations. "Let me ask you a question, Roy. What's the dress code for dinner at a country inn around here?"

"These days, there are no dress codes," said Roy. "People wear the damndest things. But a city slicker your age, you need a sport coat." Roy added to the order a tweed sport coat and a shirt and trousers to boot. Fortunately, the sport coat and trousers did not need altering, and Salt walked out with those. "Come back for the suit at four thirty," hollered Roy as Salt walked out of the store.

CHAPTER NINETEEN

Small Town America Issues III

Salt really didn't need a haircut, but he could get to be a shaggy mess by the time he got back from a week in London if he didn't get a trim. He dropped in at Georgie's to see what the wait was like. All of the barbers were busy, and it would take an hour or so for his number to come up, so he said he would take a number and come back later in the afternoon. He noticed that "College Basketball Today" was on the TV on the wall and drawing a lot of attention. The extra chairs were still stacked in the corner, so there was room for social distancing. Indeed, the barbershop seemed to have almost as many full seats as the arena where the game was being played. "What time do you suggest I show up?" Salt asked.

"Best to show up when the noon game is over, so aim for three thirty," said Georgie.

When Salt got back after having some lunch, Max was the first barber to be available, so Salt climbed into his chair and asked for a trim. The shop was full of patrons who had gotten their hair cut (or not) and were there to watch and comment on the game, as if the barbershop were a spin-off of Buffalo Wild Wings that required masks to be worn. There wasn't much interest in the new game that had just come on, so the chitchat focused on the first game and how bad it was; which was more corrupt, Duke or North Carolina; why the high school basketball coach had not been fired ("haven't had a decent coach since Matt Hatcher"); the nutty impact of social distancing on college athletics; and then, of course, politics.

The consensus on the new president was "wait and see." The crowd recognized that the president had been positioned as a middle-of-the-roader, but folks were perceptive and recognized that presidents seemed to go through at least four policy stages: (1) what it took to survive the primaries and get the nomination; (2) what it took to win the general election; (3) what emerged during the first hundred days as reality set in; and (4) what it took to get reelected. Max was of the view that the country needed to give Evans a chance, but Max was a bit further to the left than the consensus view. Georgie agreed with him. Don, the retired NRA member who Salt had met during his last visit to Georgie's and was pretty clearly there to watch the big-screen TV, was not a fan of the new president. "I just don't trust the new president," Don explained. "This new crew will want to take away our guns."

Georgie laughed. "Don, give me the name of a single politician who you have ever trusted."

Don smiled. "Well, Georgie, you got a point there."

"So, Mr. Deep State," Georgie said, turning to Salt, "where do you come out on the new president? Did you vote for Evans?"

"Don't let him trick you into talkin' too much," piped up Ellen, the third barber. "It's none of his business. He'll trap you if you're not careful. He preys on newcomers."

"I voted for the president," said Salt. "In my mind, there was really no choice. But I got there because I think the president is more of a moderate than most think, and I bet most of your customers are more moderate than they think of themselves as being. You have to look at that question holistically."

"What does that mean?" asked Don, the hunter.

Salt responded with some trepidation. "Well, for example, I bet that most people in here believe that the government spends too much and are worried about the national debt, especially after the humongous amount we have spent and are continuing to spend in connection with COVID-19."

"Right," said Don.

"Exactly," said Salt. "It is conservative thinking that many moderates share. Now, let's go to your concern about the president taking your guns. Do you think the Second Amendment gives you the right to own a tank?"

"Nope," said Don, without having to think for very long.

"How about a shoulder-mounted heat-seeking missile launcher?"

"Hmm," said Don, "closer call but probably not."

"Okay," said Salt. "How about a bazooka?"

"Nope."

"Colt .45 pistol?"

"Absolutely protected," said Don.

"I agree with you, Don," Salt announced, "and I would put your Remington hunting rifle and your shotgun in the same category. Where we probably run into disagreements is on assault rifles."

"Correct," commented Don.

Salt decided to push a bit. "But you see, we agree on as much or more as we disagree on. And I would bet that your concern is really not so much assault rifles as it is your lack of trust. You think if they can get a ban on assault rifles, they won't stop there and will go after your shotgun."

"Not saying," stated Don firmly.

"My point is that most of us are more in agreement than disagreement on big issues. Those who you can't say that about are extremists," Salt commented. Then he asked, "Georgie, can I take those flyers off your bulletin board?"

"Okay, I guess, Mr. Deep State. Half of them are about events that happened weeks ago anyhow."

"Thanks," said Salt. He interrupted his haircut, got out of the chair, and walked over to a cork bulletin board that was about thirty-six inches wide and twenty inches high. After removing the flyers from the bulletin board, he pulled out a pushpin and stuck it in the middle of the bulletin board. He explained, "Imagine that this bulletin board is a football field where we place players based on how far left or right they are, politically speaking. In the aggregate—that is, taking into account a whole range of issues—I place myself right on the fifty-yard line. Well, let's make it the forty-five-yard line, or five yards to the left. I'm in the middle on most issues. I bet if you ask your customers to place themselves on this field with a pushpin when nobody is watching, most will be between the thirty-five-yard lines. Not all, but most. Why not try it for a month and see? Call it a new form of political football." He headed back to the barber chair.

"I'll think about it," said Georgie. "But you have to tell us who you are. The more I listen to your smooth talk, I think you must be an agent of the Trilateral Commission or maybe something worse."

"There have been lots of conspiracy theories about the Trilateral Commission over the years." Salt smiled. "If you want to worry about organizations with dangerous influence, focus on the incredibly well-funded political action groups—on both the right and left politically—that are funded by the very wealthy and are hoarding millions today after the *Citizens United* Supreme Court decision."

"I think you avoided my question," said Georgie.

"Sorry," said Salt. "The truth just is not very exciting. I'm a lawyer who just retired from a law firm in Washington and previously spent some time in the government. You can Google me, but you won't find much more than that."

Max finished with Salt, and Salt got out of the chair. "Sorry I have to run, but I enjoyed the conversation. Try the bulletin board thing. I think it would be interesting. But be fair on how you explain it."

Ellen said, "We'll make sure he's fair about the political football game."

As he was leaving, Salt added, looking at Max, "By the way Max, that's a good sign you have there in the corner. Good for you." Max did not say anything but smiled and nodded toward Salt.

Salt then asked Georgie, "By the way, how is Hair-i-Care doing?"

"There could be a new Hair-i-Care application the next time you come in, but you still won't qualify." Georgie smiled as Salt hustled out to pick up his new suit from Roy. He also needed to clean up his car.

Don left Georgie's right after Salt and called the same number he had called after his first encounter with Salt at the barbershop. The other party asked, "What's up?"

Don responded, "The new ex-fed was back at Georgie's today, spouting off on gun control, left-wing zealots, and all manner of things. He tries to make himself seem harmless, but he don't fool me none. I think this guy could be trouble down the road. I still doubt that he's undercover FBI, but it's hard to tell for sure."

"Okay, thanks," said the other party. "I'll have some homework done on him and get back to you. But stay away from him and don't create any trouble until we decide who and what this guy really is. Maybe this is a false alarm. What's his name again?"

Don thought for a moment. "He goes by Salt Pepper, but I guess his real first name is Staunton or Stan or something like that. Remember he was a lawyer in the swamp in DC."

"Okay—thanks," said the other party, "but tell me more about the discussion." After listening to Don, the other party said, "Sounds to me like this guy is just a Goddamned liberal who escaped from DC. He won't get in the way of us demonstrating against more COVID-19 lockdowns. Stay cool until you hear back from me."

CHAPTER TWENTY

Food for Thought; Small Town America Issues IV

Salt was wearing his new sport coat and trousers when he picked up Margie for dinner. Under her winter coat, Margie was in an attractive dress and sweater, probably a little dressier than Salt's new outfit, but he was no judge of that stuff.

Margie guided Salt through about eight miles of back roads in the winter-evening darkness to a bed-and-breakfast that also had a restaurant. On the drive there, Margie had to focus on giving driving instructions, so there was no need to worry about awkward conversation pauses. When they arrived, the dining area reminded Salt of the Inn at Little Washington but less fancy. It had a log cabin feel and look, but like everyone else, they had to spread out the tables to comply with social distancing guidelines. The restaurant was not full, and masks were few and far between.

Margie broke the ice after they were seated on opposite ends of the table and had settled on a bottle of white. "Well, this isn't a first date, but it feels a little like one. Thanks for the payback on dinner; I hope you like this place. This is neither DC nor the Inn at Little Washington."

"You're welcome," replied Salt. "It's been a very long time since I had dinner with someone who wasn't a client or colleague or someone with an agenda. Plus, I'm on the introverted end of the scale unless I'm delivering messages. And I'm sure the food here will be fine. I'm just glad it's quiet."

"Well," said Margie, "introverted is okay, as I share that trait and am able to endure silence. I just hope you're not delivering messages tonight."

"No messages, but I do have some questions."

"Okay, you go first, but then I get my turn. But before we get into Q and A, maybe we should look at the menu. The seafood here is usually pretty good."

Salt started the Q and A before they could order. "So, you've been here a long time, and I've been gone for a lifetime. I'm the functional equivalent of a newcomer. What makes this town tick? Is it surviving? And what kinds of people are here now? Why do they stay?"

"Wow," said Margie. "That is a half dozen questions, and they're hard. Let's start with something easy—the population is about thirty thousand and holding pretty steady. There are good and not so good parts of town, but none of it is ugly. There needs to be some investment in the downtown, and you worry about more and more empty stores and houses that are in danger of falling into disrepair. I don't know if we'll ever really recover from COVID-19 and this recession. There is no discernable movement from the DC area into Carterville. People were still moving out to the outer edges of town when they could, and then the places where they spent money changed. But very few people are moving these days.

"This town is pretty diverse in lots of ways, including racially," Margie explained. "The people are farmers, small town merchants, workers in some light manufacturing businesses, most of which are somewhere in the automobile-manufacturing supply chain and worried about that, and some giant distribution facilities out off of Interstate 81, folks who work at Target and Walmart on the edge of town, and people who work in a wide range of positions at the college and the hospital. The college and the hospital are by far the largest employers. You heard from Dr. Greene at dinner at my place that the college is worried about enrollment in the near term and the related long-term trends, but the hospital seems to be solid. Maybe it's because we're all getting older. We're lucky to have a good community hospital and the college. They provide a good base and attract sound citizens."

Margie paused for a sip of wine and then continued. "This is not the most sophisticated place in the world, but a lot of the people here care about the community and have values that are important. They watch out for one another. The schools are not superb, but they're solid. Church membership is slumping as the baby boomers thin out, but likely better than in most places, and the churches are active. Bottom line—this is a good place to live. Many people value diversity, and the others put up with it, and most could not do much better if they moved. This is an ecosystem that works—at least for now.

"By the way," Margie inserted carefully, "speaking of churches, you would be more than welcome at our church. It's none of my business, but to quote President George W. Bush in a conversation with David Gregory, 'How's your faith?'"

"Hmm," responded Salt, "that's a far-out question. Truth is, I haven't figured that out. It's something I need to think about and sort out for myself. If there is a God—he or she wasn't there for my wife when she was dying, and my wife was a really good person. She was a Christian in every sense of the word. I haven't gotten over that yet, and I'm not sure I will."

"Well," Margie said, "sorry I brought that up, but if you ever want to talk about it, there are people here who would be glad to do that. But enough on that topic."

Salt thought for a few moments and decided to change the subject. "Going back to the local hospital, I was interested to learn at your dinner party that the local hospital seems to be thriving. That's a good sign as well as a good thing. Has it been hammered by opioid overdoses, or has this community been able to avoid that crisis? And how has it held up under the coronavirus stress?"

"I honestly don't know the answer to the opioid question, and my guess is that the hospital doesn't talk much about that kind of thing. I would be glad to introduce you to the president of the hospital, but he's pretty tight-lipped. Or you could talk to the editor of the local newspaper, which now comes out only three days per week. The editor is very smart and inquisitive; you would almost certainly end up telling her more about you than you would get out of her."

"Never mind. I'll take a long-term rain check on meeting the editor," said Salt, "though I don't have much about me that would be interesting to the media. How has the hospital done during the coronavirus challenge?"

"We were pretty lucky," said Margie. "Last year we had about seventy-five hospitalized cases and eighteen or so deaths. The hospital was able to handle the load, though I hear they're still waiting for the promised federal money for the no-pay stays they had. Our health care team was great.

"The diversity of this area extends to political views, as you may have picked up during your barbershop visits," added Margie. "There was likely a strong contingent of people who held their noses and voted for President Pope in the last election. Down deep, a majority are moderates politically for the most part, and they were offended by candidates who seemed to question the importance of normal folks. It would be hard to characterize this as flyover country, but we don't think of ourselves as members of either the East Coast elite or what some referred to in 2016 as the deplorables. We think nobody is deplorable—with the possible exception, for some of us, of former President Pope."

Salt asked, "How do people feel about the new president?"

"Most of us think the jury is still out on Evans," responded Margie. "On domestic issues, the president looks, feels, and acts a bit like a socialist in moderate's clothing. You know the line: if it looks like a duck, walks like a duck, and quacks like a duck, it's a duck. Evans said what was necessary to get elected. Foreign policy is not something I've thought a lot about. But most of us want to bring our troops home and repair bridges here rather than in the Middle East."

Margie added, "Sorry if I offended you anywhere in there, but you asked. I don't normally go on like this. Time for me to have some wine and shut up. But we need to order first."

The masked waiter appeared, and they each ordered the crab dip appetizer, a small Caesar salad, and the venison house special for the evening. Salt thought for a few seconds about how this meal would compare to what he would be having in London in a few days, but he didn't go there in the discussion.

"I agree with you on the local political climate," Salt said. He went on to describe his unscientific political football game experiment at Georgie's barbershop. He wondered out loud how fairly the game would be described, as it was definitely a game in which the rules determined the outcome.

"I give you credit for even thinking about trying that," said Margie. "You had to be ready for verbal abuse; that took guts."

"Time will tell about that, but striving for moderation and collaboration is a cause for me. Now, tell me about the farmers here. It seems like things are tight."

Margie responded between bites of the appetizer. "Yes, things have been tight ever since President Pope created havoc in the grain markets with the tariffs on China, and the recession only made things worse. As you know, I'm not a farmer, but I know many of those folks, and based on what I hear, many of the local farmers were stretched when the tariffs were imposed, and things got worse when China, in particular, imposed its own grain tariff and quota system and stopped buying as much US grain, and then the coronavirus hit. The government provides some subsidies, but nobody wants a handout. And nobody thinks the new normal will be as good as the pre-COVID-19 normal. Once you change buying patterns, they're changed."

Salt pressed on. "How about manufacturing? Any impact there from things international? Domestic US manufacturing has been in a mild recession since sometime in 2019."

Margie responded, "I don't really know. My impression is that the uncertainty created by the China trade issues and, for a while, the process of replacing NAFTA with the US-Mexico-Canada trade agreement threw a wrench into things, so to speak, and of course things got a lot worse in 2020. Yes, uncertainty no doubt has a cost. But the strikes that took place with several auto worker unions a year and a half ago also had an impact here in the form of lost income. It seems to me that our trade policy ought to be focused on increasing what we sell overseas and job creation and security. Wasn't that what Pope was preaching when he was elected? I sometimes wonder how he defined a *good deal*. But maybe that's just me.

"Now," she said. "I've already told you that I know nothing about foreign policy and am not really that interested in it. Yet, here we are, and it's your turn to talk and stop asking questions. What is it that you do again? After the party at my house, several people came away thinking you had answered that question, but then they thought about it and realized you had said nothing."

"Guilty." Salt laughed. "The reality is that I don't know what I do. As I think I've told you, I spent the past five years practicing law, primarily in the trade area. Nothing unusual or exciting, but we tried to get rid of wasteful blockages where we could, or open doors to new trade in other cases. Prior to that, I was in the State Department and Treasury and was essentially working on the same issues as when I practiced law—just from a different perspective. When I moved out here, I had assumed I would retire, certainly from the practice of law, and probably from everything else. An old friend of mine in the government called me last week and asked me to take on a short-term consulting gig, and I'm going to do that I think, though the parameters are not yet defined—except that I can't say much more about it. It will involve some travel, and I had to go to Roy's men's shop this afternoon to upgrade my wardrobe a bit. I expect to be gone for a week or so. I have Jack Davis looking after things on the farm while I'm gone."

"I'm glad you and Jack are getting along," Margie said. "It's none of my business, but from what I hear, he'll need some help to get back on his financial feet. He's a good guy, so thanks. But now back to you. You just created as many questions as you answered, but I won't badger you with more questions about what you'll be doing. Sounds like it would be a waste of time. But what do you think? You are now what amounts to the local guru on things political. How do you feel about the new president and how all of that is going to work?"

Salt responded, "Oh, I'm no guru. And I'm not sure how the new president will work out. I'm more moderate than the president seems—at least based on the election campaign debate rhetoric and what the president has said. I'm squarely in the middle on most issues. I'm concerned about the new administration on a number of fronts. But the president also has to get things through Congress, which until recent times has involved compromise. I guess I'm as interested in what is doable with the new administration and Congress as I am about where the president stands on theoretical issues. So I guess paint me hopeful but guarded. I'm virtually certain that I'll see pretty much eye-to-eye with the new administration on foreign relations. My bigger concern is what's happening on the domestic front."

At this point, the server signaled that the main course was almost ready, so they finished the appetizer and switched to red wine to drink with the venison.

"Foreign relations sounds pretty exotic to those of us out here in the sticks," said Margie. "And complicated."

"Yes and no," said Salt. "It's less complicated than you think. In the final analysis, people all over the world want what's best for their families and their countries, and in most cases, they would trade positions with an American in a second. We need to remember how fortunate we are and that—with some exceptions—human nature tends to favor the same basic goals all around the world. There are lots of complicating factors that get in the way, like greed and hunger for power, but in my experience, those diseases do not infect everyone."

"On that hopeful note," Margie said, "let's order dessert early so you can get home at a decent hour and unpack a few more boxes tomorrow before you start packing your bag."

"Good idea," said Salt, grateful to be left off the hook in terms of answering more questions.

CHAPTER TWENTY-ONE

London

Salt did spend Sunday unpacking more boxes, adding to his giveaway pile, and thinking about what he needed to pack for London. There had been a time when he traveled enough that even international travel had become routine. But that was years ago.

Salt got a good start on Monday morning—while it was still dark—so he could easily make the morning flight from Dulles International to London Heathrow airport. The grief he would take if he missed the flight would be unimaginable, starting (but not ending) with Louise. It was a good thing he started early because Interstate 66 was a mess with what they called in the Washington area a "wintery mix"—which in the real world meant nothing, but in the DC area, it meant big traffic issues, and of course Louise beat him to the lounge on concourse C, even with his good start.

She wisecracked about his being later than her, but fortunately neither Louise nor Salt was a morning person, so they were both mostly content to read the paper and the latest *Economist* while waiting to board. And of course, there wasn't much they could talk about on the flight on the way over. The seats in economy (not business class of course) were in a two-three-two configuration with seven seats per row and two aisles. Salt and Louise were in one of the two-seat pairs near the window, but even in a rather empty plane with no middle seats occupied, there was not nearly enough privacy to allow for a substantive discussion, especially since one had to basically yell through one's mask to be heard. Flight attendants and passengers alike were provided with and required to wear masks while on board the plane.

Salt spent a good portion of the seven-hour flight trying to get his head around the fact that he was on the flight at all and how the discussions with Peter Banks of the British Foreign and Commonwealth Office should open up. Salt tentatively settled on using some of the concepts from the Napkin B discussion with Stuart for openers.

Louise was also focused on the Peter Banks meeting but to some extent occupied herself by trying again to figure out Salt. He seemed simple at some levels but was also complicated. As to the meeting with the Brits, she was willing to go with a variation of the Napkin B outline.

After landing in London and gathering their baggage—at about 10:00 p.m. London time—Salt asked through his mask if Louise wanted to take an Uber to the hotel.

Louise responded crisply, "Never leave an unnecessary trail when traveling. Cabs are the most anonymous, the Heathrow Express train is next, and car service charges leave too much of an electronic trail. And keep in mind that there are cameras everywhere, especially in London."

They made their way down to the Heathrow Express train in the lower level of the terminal and were fortunate not to have to wait too long before boarding. Salt had a genuine fondness for London, but the relatively short train trip to London's Paddington Station in the dark was anything but scenic. When they arrived at Paddington in the late evening, the station was nearly empty—a good thing since that meant the queue for a cab wasn't very long. They queued up in the line for a black London cab, noticed the near uniform use of masks in the station, and after getting to the front of the line made it through the mostly empty streets of London without incident. They eventually (a little after 11:00 p.m.) arrived at the Marriott at

Grosvenor Square, near the former US embassy. Thankfully, Louise took care of checking them in, since she knew what names and credit cards they were using for the two rooms.

Fortunately, the bar at the hotel was still open—not always the case in London—and they were able to chat for a few minutes in the quiet, though Louise reminded Salt that the walls of a bar this close to the former US embassy could still have ears, and they needed to be careful. She commented that she was surprised that Stuart would spend so much on a hotel for them, especially one that could leak. Salt could not decide whether he thought Louise was nuts or cautious. It didn't matter, as they would be playing by her rules. The rationale for Stuart's hotel choice became clearer when a fellow by the name of Ed Jordan, who held a nondescript title with the US embassy, joined their table at a social distance and suggested another round.

Louise knew Jordan from a prior encounter, but Salt knew nothing of him. Jordan explained, "I know damn little about who you are, Salt. I don't know what you're doing here, how long you'll be doing it, how Louise is involved, or whether any of whatever you're up to makes sense. My orders are to serve as a liaison for you, help when asked if it's a reasonable request, not mention you to anyone in London, and stay the hell out of the way and out of trouble."

"Glad to make your acquaintance, Ed," said Salt, "and we'll get along just fine since I know just a smidgen more than you do about what we're doing here." Jordan knew that comment meant that Salt and Louise would not be talking, so the chatter turned social and was rather short-lived. They exchanged contact information and broke up. Louise and Salt were getting ready to deal with the jet lag when trying to get some sleep. At least the BBC news was on the *telly*.

Neither slept well, and the next morning they ran into each other in the restaurant at eight o'clock. It wasn't crowded—a good thing since the seating was spread out. Each had the traditional English breakfast but with lots of coffee rather than tea. Salt asked Louise what she knew about Ed Jordan. The answer was virtually nothing. They decided to minimize contact with him. They then exchanged views on how the meeting with the Brits should go and then left for the meeting via an anonymous black cab.

It was rush hour in London, but even in the UK, which had developed more control over COVID-19 than the United States, the lingering effects of the pandemic were still apparent. This was visible in the auto and foot traffic and the many face masks and social distance between pedestrians. Salt didn't mind very much the slow traffic. He enjoyed the look and feel and history of London and was disappointed that skyscrapers were beginning to dominate the skyline of the area called the City and Canary Wharf in particular. Salt, being a traditionalist, preferred lower buildings with less glass. He particularly enjoyed the Whitehall and Westminster areas. But he knew that his traditionalism would have to give way to the cost benefits of taller buildings; he would just have to get over it. He commented to Louise that he was thankful for the height restrictions that still existed in the District of Columbia.

Even with the reduced traffic, the pace was slow as they crept from the hotel to the British Foreign and Commonwealth Office on King Charles Street, near St. James Park and Churchill's War Rooms. They arrived on time (which is to say ten minutes early), had their temperatures taken, were issued fresh masks, and were shown into a lovely, very formal conference room that no doubt had a wonderful history. If only those silk-covered walls could talk. They were joined in a few minutes by Peter Banks and three of his colleagues—a diverse group of millennials.

Peter was nothing if not polite in a perfectly British manner. He was also exactly how one would picture an experienced UK diplomat—straight out of central casting. He was probably 5'10", on the thin side, with black hair, and was wearing an impeccable dark blue suit and traditional tie. He no doubt attended the *right* schools. After the necessary introductions, which were a bit more condensed than normal, Peter opened up and got to the point: "I hope you don't mind that we have been joined by a few of my colleagues. Stuart did not give us a perfectly clear picture of your mission, so it was hard to know who ought to be in our meeting. I can assure you, however, that none of the lips in this room are loose, and these are some of our most thoughtful folks."

"Thanks, Peter," responded Salt. "That's perfect, for we're not entirely clear on how to describe our mission. Saving the world order would sound a bit grandiose, but it's not too far off."

Salt continued. "With the understanding that we're all colleagues in the art of foreign relations and operating under the proverbial cone of silence, let me be direct. There are some in the new US administration, including the president, who are painfully aware that the world order has deteriorated in no small part due to lack of attention from, and respect for, the United States. We all recognize that the world order put together by figures such as Churchill and FDR during and after World War II could not survive without change, and a great deal of change has been accommodated over the years. But pressure for realistic accommodation has in some cases diluted a focus on the greater good in favor of attempts to misuse or circumvent multilateral institutions that have served us well. Some of this is due to ego, some to ignorance leading to predictable mistakes, some to budget priorities, and some to bad faith. We need not sort all of that out for our purposes. We acknowledge that, depending on one's politics, these developments could be viewed as including things like the United States' recent nationalistic tendency to bash NATO and the UK's troubled exit from the EU.

"Rightly or wrongly, we believe that although the United States has been part of the solution for the most part after World War II, it has become an element of the problem in recent years. However, we also believe we can—over time and with proven good works—once again assume a constructive leadership role in the world. We do not presume that the role played by the United States during the Cold War can be reestablished, nor could that be sold in the United States. But we think it is in the interest of most of the world for the United States to become again more constructively engaged. We need to trade isolationism in for what some refer to as inclusive multilateralism. We seek the input of carefully selected allies as to what role makes sense for America, what are the barriers, and whether these allies might be willing—over time—to be openly supportive.

"Our new president seeks to restore some elements of a democratic world order, but the president is painfully aware of the recent behavior of the United States and that, as a new and untested player on the world scene, the president is not in a position to go very far out on a limb here. In other words, the president is willing to take the risk of leadership if others support the United States in such a role, but not the risk of being stabbed in the back or accused of folly. And of course this can't be viewed as a power grab by the United States, because is it not that—though many will refuse to accept that proposition.

"We are here in a first meeting of this type to learn whether there are shared concerns on the part of the UK, and—if there is interest in joining in efforts to rebuild genuine multilateralism—how to prioritize efforts and issues and what role the United States should play over time. Not to put too fine a point on it, if we can't identify shared concerns and willingness to participate between the United States and the UK, there is not much sense in pursuing this further with others. This is not to attempt to place undue pressure on the UK, but the reality is that we do need to understand whether others think we're just plain nuts to try to put back together Humpty Dumpty, when we know we were involved in pushing poor Humpty off the wall."

Salt paused. Peter Banks smiled. Everyone was speechless for a few moments. Peter finally broke the silence. "Well, I wasn't sure what to expect, but it was not this. The proposition is unusual to say the least, and the whole subject is more than slightly above our pay grades. To put it in military terms, this is something that needs to be discussed with generals, and we are privates. I think it would be a mistake for us to respond at all right now. We have this group on our side of the table available this afternoon. Rather than trying to formulate a response on an off-the-cuff basis, I suggest we hit the pause button and allow our group to talk among ourselves and perhaps a few others. We could then reassemble briefly after lunch for an initial response and decide what else, if anything, makes sense at this time. It may be that we just can't deal with this at all in a short time frame. What you have outlined is not unambitious, to say the least. In any event, we hope you can join a few of us for a private dinner this evening here in Whitehall."

"That is more than reasonable," said Salt. "But I'm a little concerned that I have not stated our case either fully or very well."

"I think we get enough of it," said Peter. "You were more than articulate. And besides, this is the type of topic that you talk about initially for either forty minutes or forty hours. We don't have time for the forty-hour version."

"When should we return?"

"Let's aim for two o'clock," said Peter.

CHAPTER TWENTY-TWO

London: Further Reflections

As Salt and Louise were leaving, walking down the steps in front of the British Foreign and Commonwealth Office, Salt opened up and said, chuckling, "I'm pretty sure we were just thrown out of the British Foreign and Commonwealth Office on our asses, but I can't tell whether they were horrified or laughing. But it was all very polite. How the hell am I going to explain this to the president and Stuart Bacon?"

"Don't worry about what you'll need to say to the president," said Louise. "If this is not going anywhere, Stuart will blame you in absentia, and you won't get a chance to explain anything to the president. But I'm not sure the Brits won't experiment, at least a little bit. Though they will likely want it in small bites and be able to maintain at all times plausible deniability."

"Time will tell," said Salt. "I need to take a quiet walk and think about things. Why don't we meet back here at 1:50 p.m. and then reenter the lion's den."

"Fine by me," said Louise.

It was a typically gray and damp winter day in London but not raining. Salt took his walk around the nearby areas of London. Since they were in the neighborhood, he walked slowly by Westminster Abbey and Parliament and even got nearly as far as Buckingham Palace. As he walked, he decided that he may as well be optimistic and think about what he would say to the Brits in the Foreign and Commonwealth Office about next steps. He pulled out of his suit coat pocket his wrinkled version of Napkin B from their discussion with Stuart and the president. He read it again:

1. Stuart Bacon is secretary of state.
2. Pepper reports directly to Bacon and President Evans, including reasonable direct access to Evans.
3. In G-7 and other selected countries, a direct contact in the US embassy, acceptable to Pepper, will be established with such contacts reporting solely to Pepper and the secretary of state with respect to this project; project not to be shared with political appointees.
4. Good faith attempts to rejoin Paris Climate Accord.
5. Good faith attempts to rejoin TPP.
6. Much more limited and targeted use of tariffs.
7. Strong support of NATO, not to foreclose pressure on member state defense spending.
8. Approach to North Korea to be closely coordinated with allies, especially South Korea and Japan.
9. Approach to Iran to be closely coordinated with allied parties to the Iran nuclear treaty the US withdrew from (Joint Comprehensive Plan of Action), and stay out of wars in the Middle East.
10. Commitment to strengthen professional senior staffing at State Department.
11. Rapid movement toward renewed New START talks without requiring China to participate.
12. Fix Ukraine mess.

He mentally added the WHO and global health issues to his

version of the list. He also realized that he had thrown the New START treaty back into the mix.

He recalled that the president had said that the list was for discussion and not sharing, and also that the president said the new administration could not yet live with comprehensive immigration reform. After thinking more about it, he decided he would talk to Louise about orally walking the Brits through appropriate items—assuming they had any interest.

At the appointed hour, Salt and Louise arrived back at the Foreign and Commonwealth Office and met again with Peter Banks and team. They were all in stiff upper lip mode and difficult to read.

After niceties, Peter Banks opened the discussion. "First," Banks said, "we appreciate very much your visit and the interesting concept underlying the discussion. As you can understand, at this point we're not high enough in the food chain to do more than listen and react, and this group could not sign up for anything. In addition to getting others involved, there needs to be meat on the bones here. However, in principle, we are supportive to some undefined extent and, subject to some reasonable conditions, willing to continue discussions."

"Well," Salt said, laughing, "that has to be a finalist for the most caveats of all time. Want to add any more?"

Banks also quietly laughed, saying, "I knew you would get the message."

"Okay," said Salt, "what are the conditions?"

Peter responded: "In no particular order:

"Until we advise to the contrary, the UK is not to be referred to as being involved, much less supportive. To be frank, we were burned more than once by your prior administration, and it will take time to restore trust, if it can be restored at all. This will take actual experience. No amount of talk will get there.

"You may disclose discretely to a preapproved list of governments that we have discussed the subject and are willing to think about it, but no more than that.

"We have to agree to some core foundational elements that give the discussion more substance. This is essential. If we can't identify shared goals at the outset, we're out.

"We need to be kept up to date on discussions with others. We don't want veto power over who you talk to or daily updates, but we need veto power over who you talk to about us being possibly involved and how.

"We have the right to withdraw from the discussions at any time and for any reason."

Salt looked at Louise for silent assent and got it, so he responded. "Those are all fair enough and agreed to," said Salt. "I share the trust issues myself. In response to your need for more substance, allow me to read to you a summary of a few of the points we have discussed with the president and Stuart Bacon. I need to emphasize that that these are both partial and preliminary." At that point, Salt in effect converted much of the Napkin B content into guiding principles and goals, reading slowly off his list so the Brits could take notes:

- good faith attempts for the United States to rejoin Paris Climate Accord
- good faith attempts for the United States to rejoin Trans-Pacific Partnership
- much more limited and targeted use of tariffs and unilateral economic sanctions
- strong and collaborative support of NATO, not to foreclose continued pressure on member state defense spending
- approach to North Korea to be closely coordinated with allies, especially South Korea and Japan
- new approach to Iran to be closely coordinated with allies, particularly parties to the Iranian Joint Comprehensive Plan of Action that was abandoned by our prior president
- thoughtful and collaborative approach to the Ukraine challenges
- United States stays out of Brexit and related issues (other than US-UK trade treaty discussions)—those are for the UK and the EU to resolve

Salt concluded by saying that there were a few other items that did not make this short list but were important. These included the US relationship with the WTO and WHO. He also emphasized that the United States was glad to entertain suggestions from the UK.

"An interesting list," said Peter. "But back to the issue of why are you here, rather than your secretary of state, and why me and my team rather than our foreign secretary?"

Salt took a deep breath and responded, "I have the same question at some level. As we discussed this morning, we have to acknowledge that the United States has suffered significantly diminished credibility around the world, whether dealing with friend or foe. We are viewed as volatile, xenophobic, isolationist, unreliable, and untrustworthy. The lack of trust is deep and a serious problem. We have reluctantly concluded that people viewed as political appointees, or otherwise closely allied with the new administration, will not be as effective as such persons have been in the past, no matter who they are. What they say to others in the world will be treated as more blah, blah, blah. And what they say will stand only for as long as that person is around, at best. The goal is to get these topics more fully into the hands of smart, trusted, and apolitical senior career diplomats who can work on this in the background without being forced prematurely to disclose the nature and status of the project. We report to Stuart Bacon and the president.

"As to why you and your team," Salt continued, "my understanding is that Stuart and your foreign secretary agreed on the composition of the teams. I don't know what the specs were."

"Well, your candor is valued, if that is what this is," Peter responded. "We need to have more time to discuss this among ourselves this afternoon. Please come back again at 6:30 p.m., when we can have dinner here and, I dare say, a gin and tonic or two. I don't anticipate being able to have much in the way of further substantive discussions this evening, but perhaps we can chart next steps."

As Peter was walking Salt and Louise out, he pulled them aside and spoke quietly. "I don't want to overdo this, but you need to understand that the moment you walked in the front door today, you were probably identified as persons of possible interest to Russian intelligence. It is not something to be proud of, as we think that label applies to just about anyone who comes through the front door until proven to be not of much interest." Peter reminded them that the UK had recent experience in dealing with Russia acting covertly and aggressively within the UK's borders. In 2018, the Russian military intelligence service had poisoned a former Russian spy who lived in a small English town, as well as his daughter, with the weapons-grade nerve agent Novichok. If what Salt and Louise were proposing gained momentum, it would be of interest to the Russians, Peter emphasized, and Salt and Louise should be careful.

"Thanks, I guess," said Louise. "And here I expected that our food for thought would come this evening."

As Salt and Louise left the building, Salt looked at her and asked, "Was that for real?"

"This is not the time or place for that discussion," responded Louise. They fell silent on the way back to their hotel.

CHAPTER TWENTY-THREE

London: More Serious Chats

Upon arrival at the hotel, they went to the bar. They drank water this time. Louise said she had discussed the security of the bar with Ed Jordan of the embassy, who felt it was pretty safe until they had reason to believe that someone was focusing on them.

"Well—what do you think?" asked Salt.

Louise responded, "I guess it's about what we should have expected in an optimistic case, based on the reaction you got from your Canadian friend. We need to start somewhere, and the UK is the right place for that, I think. Peter Banks seems like a decent enough and straightforward guy. And of course the Brits have their own issues, so there is a limit on how much bashing they can dish out to us. We need to think about next steps. It feels to me like we need to pick one or two matters to focus on and hopefully start building credibility."

"Agreed," said Salt. "Let's think about that while we freshen up for dinner."

They met in the hotel lobby a few minutes after six o'clock. Louise looked like a different person. Until then, Salt had seen Louise only in a black pantsuit and white blouse. Now she was wearing a striking dress—not quite what Salt would call a cocktail dress but very tastefully colorful and snazzy just the same. And she had done things with her hair. "I'm not sure what the rules are these days," said Salt, "but I hope I won't offend you if I say that you look lovely. My only question is whether your gun fits in that small handbag."

"No offense and thank you," said Louise, "and the gun fits." She continued, "I hope I won't offend you, Salt, but is that the same shirt and tie you had on this afternoon?"

"Yes," said Salt. "What about it?"

Louise frowned and asked, "Do you have a clean shirt in your room?"

"Yes," said Salt again.

"Okay," Louise said. "You go up and put on the most heavily starched, clean white shirt you have with you. While you do that, I'm going around the corner to a men's store I saw this afternoon to get you a new tie. You have five minutes. Get going."

Eight minutes later, Louise was helping Salt with his new and much dressier tie. "There," she said. "Now you look like someone who has been to London before."

"Thanks," murmured Salt as they climbed into a cab. "Now, what do you think about where things stand now?"

Louise responded, "You're right; we need to have a very short list of goals. It needs to be something that will garner the UK's attention for other reasons. And it needs to be something that we think we can quickly make progress on. We need an early-stage win if at all possible."

"Completely agree," said Salt. "Let's see what they come up with."

They arrived back at the Foreign and Commonwealth Office and were met by Peter Banks's young male assistant, who was the essence of propriety and care while he took their temperatures. He followed carefully all of the relevant protocols. They were taken to another very formal and ornate meeting room, complete with silk wall coverings and huge glass chandeliers, where the Foreign and Commonwealth team was assembling and having their traditional gin and tonic while maintaining social distance but foregoing masks. The conversation was light and stayed that way through a traditional British dinner of lamb or dover sole, touching upon subjects such as the Royals, COVID-19 and the failure of both countries to handle it well, US state and local politics, comparisons of the House of Commons and the US Congress, developments in Hong Kong and elsewhere in Asia, the last-second avoidance of a no-deal Brexit with the completion at the end of December of the UK-EU trade treaty, and the Black Lives Matter movement in the United States and the UK, including the significant demonstrations in London. Over dessert and coffee and tea, they debated whether Winston Churchill was a racist. That discussion continued later and required an after-dinner cordial.

Peter led off for the Brits after dessert, gaining attention by standing and carefully pinging his empty glass. "Salt and Louise, we have been thinking about our earlier discussion. We are not backing away from what we said, but we feel honor bound to emphasize how difficult this will be. It is possible to destroy a country's reputation in a very short period of time based on a few issues. It is much more difficult to restore mutual trust and confidence, and the restoration efforts need to focus on issues important to both of us. Progress on petty issues won't cut it. The more we think about it, the more we think this effort is what you Yanks call a very heavy lift that will take a long time. If we proceed, we need to manage the expectations of our respective leaders."

Louise spoke up, agreeing with Peter's overview. Continuing, she explained, "Peter, we think we need to identify one or two matters that are important enough to generate the needed level of attention, are in the land of the doable, and are not so complicated that it's likely to take years to develop trust around those matters."

"Do you have anything in mind?" asked Peter.

"We have a couple items to bounce off of you," Louise responded.

Salt was pleased that Louise was stepping up and taking the initiative, and he was impressed and kept his mouth shut.

Louise continued. "The post-Brexit US-UK trade negotiations are stalled on several fronts. Let's pick two of those issues for our working group to focus on. In addition, let's focus on one or two elements of the Ukraine relationships. Now that the United States has a new administration that has not yet been burned by Ukrainian witnesses and complications, it should be easier to make progress as between our countries and then with NATO and ultimately Russia."

"Sorry to interrupt," said Peter, "but this is important. We will think about that list, which on its face seems reasonable. The US-UK trade negotiations are front of mind. To be honest, we're concerned about the United States on the trade front. We are all focused on the continuing COVID-19 crisis and whether the two vaccines that are being focused on will work and how fast, as well as the effects of the continuing recession. Our economists see US manufacturing as being in trouble. And the United States does not have left many domestic tools to deal with these issues. You have used up most of your dry powder in the form of monetary and fiscal stimuli, and it could be tempting to blame Brexit and Europe and impose more tariffs. We and Europe would view that as a form of economic warfare. Some of us are also concerned that the supply chain lessons of the COVID-19 experience and the survival of some of the America-first theme will cause the US private sector to embrace near-shoring and invest heavily in new facilities. That could involve the use of robotics and artificial intelligence to insulate manufacturing from labor costs and make it financially feasible to move more manufacturing back to the United States."

"Fair enough," replied Salt. "But let's not forget the role of the UK and Brexit in terms of fragmenting trade and breaching alliances. We are also a bit unnerved by your politics, including your prime minister, who does not seem to have the right temperament to manage a country, and the leader of the pro-Brexit movement. We just don't know much about the new head of your Labour Party. There is quite a thick and unpredictable stew cooking in the UK as well as in the United States."

Louise leaned in. "All of us involved in this process will have to be assessing whether we think the European Union will survive the combined effect of Brexit, COVID-19, the recession, and the rise of the right around the world."

Peter concurred. "Unfortunately, all of that does have to be on our radar." Smiling, he added, "I guess you Yanks should know a leader not qualified to run a country when you see one. Who could forget the July 2018 show in Helsinki?"

Peter continued, "Returning to your list, we would have liked to add reinstating the Paris Climate Accord and the JCPOA treaty with Iran and others, but we think those are too ambitious in all kinds of ways. And the United States is not in a position to take a lead role on those. Left to our own devices, we might also add north Africa, and Libya in particular, to your list, which is really not so short any more. In any event, we need to define the parameters of our target issues in more detail and make sure we have a shared understanding of what would constitute a mutual win on those issues for our working group. Let's see if we can achieve that definition over the next week or so."

"Thanks, Peter," said Salt. "We hear you on the target issues. We will need to discuss these with Stuart tomorrow, and he will no doubt need to consult, but we will do that and revert. Hopefully we can achieve a mutual understanding soon and also agree on who should be involved. One other topic that we might put on the short list is managing global pandemics, the role of the WHO, the role of China vis-à-vis the WHO, and what else might be needed in support of the WHO. In any event, thanks for your time and thoughts today, not to mention dinner."

"You're most welcome, Salt and Louise. Let us know how Stuart reacts to what we have discussed and when you think we might kick things off. It occurs to me that we have some of the same domestic attitudes and challenges surrounding these topics. In that regard, history can be both interesting and illuminating at times, and I double-checked a couple items late this afternoon. It was on August 30, 2013, that our House of Commons refused to support our Prime Minister's request for authority to intervene in the Syrian civil war in order to respond to, among other things, the use of chemical weapons. That rejection was a first of sorts and a surprise. Two weeks later, President Obama's efforts to obtain US Congressional approval for that effort suffered the same fate, though a deal with Russia salvaged a joint effort to remove chemical weapons. Then almost three years later, on June 23, 2016, the British people approved Brexit and, in effect, more isolation. Later in the same year, the citizens of the United States elected President Pope, who became a fan of Brexit and the kinds of things it stood for, including America first, which really meant America first, last, and always. So there is an extent to which the British people and Parliament can be leading indicators of what the United States is going to do—a barometer of sorts. We need to learn from that phenomenon.

"Remember to also be alert when you leave tonight. I doubt that you have attracted much unwanted external attention yet, but it pays to be careful." Peter then smiled and added, "By the way, if as North Americans you can develop an answer to how do you solve a problem like Prince Harry, that would be a bonus. We're actually fond of the young man and his wife."

Salt and Louise intentionally started to walk back to the hotel rather than looking for a cab. After ten minutes or so, Louise asked Salt, "Does it feel to you like someone is following us?"

It was dark of course, but they were in the well-lit Whitehall area of London. Salt looked around and said, "I don't see anything unusual."

Louise quietly laughed. "It is very unlikely that you would see someone in a situation like this. Anyone who is any good would stay out of the line of sight. You have to almost feel them."

"So you feel something is amiss?" Salt asked.

"Not certain of it," said Louise. "But I just have a sense that there is someone out there watching us. Maybe what Peter said is giving me the willies. Let's grab that cab." And they did.

After arriving at the hotel, they went to Salt's room and sent an encrypted message to Stuart, asking for a window of time when they could talk on the following day. They each had a drink from the minibar, and they chatted for a few minutes.

Salt went into thoughtful mode and commented, "Thanks for

your help today. You were on point and effective. Well done. And then, if I may say so, in addition to gaining their attention with what you had to say, you nearly destroyed their level of concentration with your striking looks. As the Brits would say, 'Bloody hell!' And remind me what I owe you for the new tie."

"Thanks, Salt," said Louise. "I think we can make a good team if we work at it."

And they were off to bed.

CHAPTER TWENTY-FOUR

Off Ramp: Middle Eastern Diversion

Salt climbed out of bed at about six thirty on Wednesday morning and checked the shoe phone for emails from the United States. Nothing yet. Even though it was the middle of the night in Washington, he had been hoping to get some guidance on the short list to be proposed to Peter and his team before they lost another day. He got dressed and went to the coffee shop in the lobby for breakfast. Louise was there, back in her black pantsuit attire. "Hope you slept well last night," she said.

Salt responded, "It took me a while at first, but then I went into a good, deep sleep. I think the jet lag has worn off. How did you sleep?"

"Fine, thanks—though, like you, it took a while to get to sleep. Too much on my mind."

They then turned to the short list of post-Brexit US-UK trade issues that could be focused on with the Brits as the trial run for the relationship-building exercise. There were so many—virtually all potential trade issues between the two nations—that they decided it made more sense to defer to Peter and Stuart and their teams; they were better positioned to identify the items that were both urgent and important for the UK, and they would have a better idea of what would be relatively easy to fix. These discussions were not starting without any prior back-and-forth. Maybe they needed to get a short list from the Brits and then consult about priorities with the right players in the United States.

They also discussed a short list of Ukrainian issues and decided they would propose some things to Stuart. They didn't discuss or comment on Salt's late addition of managing global health issues. Louise did not want to touch that item.

They then turned briefly to what the next geographical target should be. France? Germany? Someplace more exotic?

As they were finishing breakfast, Salt and Louise got email messages on their shoe phones instructing them to get to a secure location where they could talk on a land line with a speakerphone. And sooner rather than later. They called Ed Jordan at the embassy and made the necessary arrangements. They then grabbed a cab and got to the US embassy by 10:30 a.m. London time—or 5:30 a.m. in Washington. Ed Jordan settled them in a secure conference room in the embassy and then graciously departed.

At 10:45 a.m. London time, the phone rang. It was Stuart and a group of about five others who were huddled around a phone. Turned out the group in the United States was in the Situation Room in the basement of the White House.

Stuart opened the call. "We're very eager to hear how things have been going in London, but we need to shift gears to look at an even higher priority.

"You two are generally aware of the JCPOA treaty with Iran and others. And we will give you a full debrief later. As you'll recall, the treaty was signed in Vienna in July 2015 by the five permanent members of the UN Security Council (China, France, Russia, the UK, and the United States), Germany, the European Union, and Iran. President Pope withdrew the United States from the treaty in May 2018. The treaty limped along until 2020, when things deteriorated, including the breakout of hostilities at varying levels among Iran, Iraq, the United States, and others. Apart from relatively minor skirmishes and continuing confusion, nothing significant happened during the balance of 2020 and the US election process. But Iran had a serious bout with the coronavirus and blamed the United States and its sanctions regime for Iran not receiving more aid and assistance to deal with the pandemic.

"President Evans campaigned on the basis that something like the JCPOA should be brought back to life. Now that President Evans is in place, Iran has just gone to Germany to say they are willing to talk, but it has to be fast and on a secure, nonpublic basis. We realize that this is beyond your remit, but we would like for you to help get this launched. And soon."

"How soon is soon?" asked Louise.

"Tomorrow," said Stuart.

Salt protested, "But we're greenhorns in this and relatively uninformed about the people and the details of how we got here. We would be in over our heads on the first day. And more important, there are really good people available at State and other places who could run circles around us."

"You'll have to run fast," acknowledged Stuart, "but you can do it. And this is just for the first steps. We need to keep this very quiet, so we need to field a very small and minimally recognizable team at first. That would be you two plus Gretchen Grant of the State Department, who was involved in the details of the JCPOA but not in a highly visible way. Maybe one or two Germans. Gretchen is getting on a flight to Berlin this evening, arriving in the morning. Step one is to meet in Berlin with the Germans, who have perhaps maintained the best relationship with Iran. We would like that to happen tomorrow, but real world it will need to be on Friday. We envision a first meeting with the Iranians next week, date and location to be determined. Are you in?"

"What do we do with the Brits if we start focusing on this rather than what we discussed with them?" Salt asked.

Stuart was forceful. "We tell them the truth. We say you have been diverted for a few days and that meanwhile, we in Washington are studying the results of the discussions you have had in London so we can get back to them soon. We cannot and will not hang them out to dry. That effort is too important."

"Holy shit, Stuart." Salt sighed. "You know we didn't sign up for this."

"Admitted," said Stuart, "but life sometimes presents challenges that are both unanticipated and important."

"Okay, let's cut to the chase and stop wasting time," Louise said, entering the fray. "Assuming we mix well with the Germans and Gretchen, we'll help get it launched."

Salt's mouth dropped wide open. He was obviously becoming agitated, and the control freak in him came to the surface. "What the fuck, boys and girls. Are you all out of your Goddamned minds? Jesus H. Christ, what is going on here?"

Stuart started to respond, but Louise cut him off. "Look, Salt, you're a Boy Scout with patriotic tendencies, and you're smart. You're eventually going to agree to do this, so let's save fifteen minutes of histrionics and start learning about this cluster. This has about the same chance of success as the half-baked shit we threw at the Brits yesterday. At your age, a good failure or two won't hurt your résumé. My diplomatic/intelligence career, on the other hand, will be baked to a crisp. In other words, get over it."

A few moments of silence followed.

Salt frowned and said, "I'm listening."

"Good," responded Stuart. "I'm turning you over to Walter Williams, who has shifted back and forth between State and the CIA in recent years but has remained focused on the issues surrounding the JCPOA and Iran. Like Gretchen, he is one of our best and most knowledgeable. Thanks, all."

Stuart jumped off the call, and Walter joined and introduced himself. Unlike Louise, Walter did not have street experience, but he was obviously plenty smart and knowledgeable.

Walter suggested, "Let's begin at the beginning." And he did.

CHAPTER TWENTY-FIVE

Iranian Backgrounder I; Tracks in the Snow

As Walter explained, the rich history of Persia goes back essentially to the beginning of time. In the 600s, the schism between the Shia and the Sunni Muslim sects in what is now Syria developed, ostensibly over different views as to who was able to interpret the Koran, descendants of Muhammad or a broader group. Persia (named Iran since 1935) is more of the Shia persuasion, with a limited view of who can interpret the Koran. What is now Iraq housed both persuasions, though Saddam Hussein was a Sunni. Some of the larger and more oil-rich countries in the Gulf area are also more of the Sunni persuasion. One need not have a degree in Middle Eastern history to conclude that the Shia/Sunni schism is deep and most likely forever lasting and must be respected. It won't go away in our time.

Even these introductory remarks generated questions, which Walter dealt with nimbly and patiently. The Shia-Sunni relationship, and which branch of the Muslim faith dominated where, were of particular interest.

After dealing with Q and A, Walter deftly skipped forward

through several centuries and many important developments. Iran was neutral in World War II but was occupied by the UK and Russia. In 1953, a military coup backed by the United States and UK overthrew an anti-Western government. Thus entered the Shah of Iran, who with his family remained in control for many years. But in 1979, the Iranian revolution took place, the Shah was overthrown, and Ayatollah Khomeini established a strong Shiite regime in the form of the Islamic Republic. The year 1979 also witnessed the US-Iran hostage crisis, which lasted for 444 days, ending in 1981 on the day Ronald Reagan was inaugurated.

Walter reminded them that since at least 1980, the Assad regime in Syria and Hezbollah in Lebanon, both Shia in persuasion, have been supported by Iran. The Iranian support of Assad has been particularly strong since 2011. The very fierce Iran-Iraq war took place from 1980 to 1988, having begun with an Iraqi invasion of Iran in 1980.

Iran stayed on the sidelines for the most part during the height of the Gulf War (Operation Desert Shield) during 1990 and early 1991, following Iraq's invasion of Kuwait and the subsequent US-led invasion of Iraq (Operation Desert Storm) in 1991.

After dealing with several questions, Walter took a breath and continued, "Iran has been directly involved in many skirmishes with the United States of varying strength over the past decade or so. These have included a variety of incidents involving the United States and Iraq and, to a lesser extent, Israel. There has also been domestic unrest in Iran from time to time, as the Iranian population does not uniformly support what amounts to a theocracy plagued with allegations of fraud and corruption. There was significant domestic unrest in Iran during 2009 and 2010. In 2014, Iran intervened in the Yemen Civil War, which is ongoing."

Walter reminded them that the situation between the United States and Iran had become more tense in 2019 with Iran launching periodic rocket attacks into Iraq, an attack on the US embassy in Baghdad in January 2020, and what some refer to as the assassination by the United States of the prominent Iranian military leader and folk hero, General Qassim Soleimani, commander of Iranian Forces (including the Quds Force of the Islamic Revolutionary Guards Corps), in a January 3, 2020, drone attack near the Baghdad airport. Concluding, Walter explained, "Ever since that event, it is fair to say that Iran, Iraq, and the United States have had an even more troubled relationship. By the end of the first quarter of 2020, it became clear that Iran would not move in the direction of serious discussions with the United States or its allies until the US presidential elections had been held. The coronavirus pandemic added significantly to Iran's internal issues and popular unrest."

After answering a host of questions, Walter called time-out, saying, "I think that's what I was supposed to cover today. We think it would be helpful for you to meet up with Gretchen Grant in Berlin tomorrow and also let us try to set up a meeting with the Germans for Friday. We were hoping to aim for Thursday, but Gretchen will be jet-lagged, and we think it makes sense for you two and Gretchen to have some time together in Berlin tomorrow evening before meeting with the Germans on Friday.

"By the way," Walter added, "Gretchen is a serious player here. She knows her stuff. She was not prominent during the 2014–2015 discussions with Iran, but she was there and has been closely following Iran ever since. And she is well respected by the Germans."

"Thanks, Walter," said Salt. "You know, a reasonable helping of history is a good thing. I used to work with a very wise man who said that, when evaluating people, it's important to follow 'tracks in the snow.' In other words, you can tell a lot about where a person, a nation, or a group is headed by understanding where they came from and what direction they are going. Following the trajectory of tracks in the snow is not foolproof but is a good start. Thus the importance of history. Something that not all political leaders understand. So, thanks."

At the completion of Walter's presentation and their questions and related discussion, it was four o'clock on Wednesday afternoon in London. Walter hung up. It had been a long call and a long day, without a lunch break.

After Walter hung up, Salt turned to Louise. "Who is this guy Walter, and does he know his stuff? He seems to know not only facts but how they fit together and influence events."

"You're right," said Louise. "He's bounced between the Agency and State, not because he's a problem but because he's brilliant. He's African American, smart as hell, works like a dog, keeps up to date, may have a photographic memory, and is reliable. He may have a little nerd in him and will never operate in the field, but nobody cares."

"Good," Salt said. "Let's make sure he stays on the team."

CHAPTER TWENTY-SIX

Walk in the Park, Talk, and More

There was just a bit of daylight left on a cold but not very damp London evening. Salt turned to Louise and said, "I think I need to find a protein bar and take a walk in Hyde Park and noodle about all of this."

Louise responded, "You take your walk. I need to take a run. How about if we meet in the hotel lobby in two hours. Your job is to talk to the concierge and get a reservation for six thirty or seven at a decent Indian restaurant within walking distance of the hotel. The Indian food is typically very good in London. Your other job is to watch your back while taking your walk and be aware of anyone tailing you. I'll call Stuart's assistant and get us on a flight to Berlin in the morning and in a hotel tomorrow evening."

"Yes, ma'am," Salt responded, "though I think the risk of me being followed is overblown."

"Better safe than sorry," said Louise. "See you in two hours."

They both needed a break, and as they thought about things, while either walking or running, no firm conclusions were reached. Salt thought about whether he should fly to Berlin in the morning or bag this whole operation and head back to the United States and the farm near Carterville. This effort was headed in a much different direction than he was led to believe at the outset.

Salt's interest was in solving trade issues in a fashion that would help ordinary Americans—like those in and around Carterville—and honoring Meredith by trying to improve global responses to health issues. He was essentially a free trader at heart. He believed it was a mistake to try to provide artificial protection to businesses and industries. Over the long haul, they had to be able to compete. But a lot of government assistance was being doled out all around the world in an effort to stem the recession. And even Salt was in favor of steps to ensure things like a level playing field, appropriate intellectual property protections, and incubation of new businesses. These kinds of issues were capable of inspiring Salt to become involved in a mission. Meeting with the Brits to discuss US-UK free trade agreements, which would inevitably affect US-EU trade agreements, also grabbed his attention. Of course the elephant in this room was China, and improving that very complicated and troubled trade relationship (or was it a war?) could have a huge impact back home. That was the sort of thing for which Salt would defer retirement.

Dealing with Iran did not promise to materially improve trade issues in the United States. The United States was essentially energy independent, and the Iran situation was a mess that really went back centuries. Iran was certainly very important, but this wasn't going to morph into Salt's sweet spot, and he was not happy about being pushed in this direction. He was concerned that he was getting pulled into inside the Beltway chaos when he really wanted to be focused on helping those outside the Beltway.

Salt eventually talked himself into thinking that one more day would not be such a big deal, though he was still peeved about how he was getting volunteered for things without any prior notice or discussion. He needed to figure out what his ejection mechanism would be. As he brooded, he blamed Stuart for the most part, though Louise was no help. But Salt also admitted to himself that there was more to Louise than he had originally thought.

While mulling over these issues, he ate his protein bar to carry him over to dinner. He didn't notice any tail, but he reminded himself that he probably would not recognize a tail unless it carried a sign saying, "It's me."

Salt and Louise met up in the hotel lobby at six thirty and reported on their assignments. Louise had flight arrangements, and Salt had the Indian dinner reservation. They walked quietly over to the restaurant and noticed immediately the staff's compliance with mask and distancing requirements when they entered.

After being seated and ordering drinks and appetizers, Salt started the discussion. "So, Louise, tell me what you think about all of this and what it means to you. What do you want to get out of this?"

"Well, that's a complicated set of questions," Louise responded, "and I thought about them on my run this afternoon. As we discussed at Helen's Place in Carterville—which seems like a very long time ago—I'm eager to get closer to the diplomatic corps in some way, so this is a giant opportunity for me if we can pull it off at any appreciable level. I understand that you and I are at different places in our lives and that to some extent I'm being selfish and using you, but it's also true that you're uncertain about what you want to do. Are you really ready for retirement in the country? You're a thoughtful guy and a patriot in your own way, but you're not ever going to go out and drive a tractor. I doubt that you're ready to hang 'em up, and down deep, so do you. I think you would go nuts."

Salt responded instinctively. "I didn't realize that you're a shrink as well as one of what my new barber calls pointy-headed members of the Deep State. But I'll admit that you're not too wrong. I'm struggling and willing to concede that to you. The stakes are very high in this particular game. To say the least, we're not the most likely duo to pull this off, and if there were not a need for virtual anonymity, we would not be sitting here. For me, it's a conundrum. If we do this, we cannot screw it up. Who needs that kind of pressure?"

"The pressure is real, I admit," said Louise, "but think how cool it would be to play even a small role in beginning to restore the United States to a place of genuine respect, influence, and moderation in the world, including in the health care arena. At some level, we're all in this to be able to do some good. Let's just do the best we can."

Louise wanted to pause the conversation there and give her comments time to sink in. She said, "Excuse me, I need to visit the ladies' water closet. Think about what we might be able to achieve, and maybe we'll even enjoy working with each other. You're not as much of a dinosaur as either of us thought." Then she was gone.

After Louise returned, they moved on to lighter conversation, finished dinner, and Salt paid the check.

As they started to walk toward the hotel, Louise asked, "Did you see those two guys in the shadows as we left the restaurant? They were just standing there when we came out of the restaurant, but now they're walking about sixty yards behind us. Let's split up. I'll take that cab over there, and you walk back. Let's see what they do."

As Louise and Salt split up, the two men stopped and talked quietly. There being no other cabs handy, they turned to follow Salt. But they kept to themselves as Salt neared the hotel. Salt now admitted to himself that Louise was right about a possible tail. But what to do about it? Nothing, Salt concluded, other than being aware and careful. Besides, they would be in Berlin by early afternoon tomorrow.

After reaching the hotel, Salt and Louise met up in the hotel bar again, and Salt disclosed his agreement with Louise as to the tail. They agreed they would mention it to Stuart on the next call that offered an opportunity. After one glass of wine, Louise abruptly stood up and kissed Salt on the head and, after looking back at Salt on her way out of the bar, went to her room without saying another word. After Louise was gone, Salt wondered what that meant and how in the hell he was going to get to sleep after that kind of a teaser.

They both went to bed thinking about things.

About an hour after they left the bar, Louise used a gizmo to pick the electronic lock on Salt's door and walked in. She still looked fabulous and was wearing very little. Without saying a word, she climbed into bed with Salt, and they became better acquainted. Louise was gone when Salt woke up on Thursday morning.

After sitting up on the edge of the bed, Salt wondered if what had happened during the night before was just a dream. It was a hell of a dream if that's what it was. But there was a psychological complication. Salt started feeling guilty, as if he were cheating on his wife. She had passed away nine months ago, but Salt remained intensely loyal to her memory, and he missed her on a daily basis. Salt honestly believed he needed to move on with his life, and that was what his wife would want. But there was still that uneasy feeling.

Salt and Louise met up in the lobby. They were both quiet when leaving the hotel in a cab and then at the airport and on the plane. There was no sign of the tail—if there was one. But Louise said she felt it in her bones.

CHAPTER TWENTY-SEVEN

Berlin Bearings

Since Brexit had not yet been fully implemented, they didn't need visas or other new travel documentation for the flight from London Heathrow to Berlin. They did need their COVID-19 test certificates. The flight was not very long, and it was surprisingly crowded, with most of the passengers wearing masks, so there was no serious talk. They grabbed a cab at the Berlin airport and, at Louise's insistence, continued to be careful about what they said in public places and the cab. Someone had trained her well.

On the way in from the airport to downtown Berlin, Salt was reminded of how interesting and diverse Berlin was and of its complicated history. Berlin had the feel of a much newer city than many other European capitals, and much of it actually was newer. It suffered serious damage during World War II and was then hampered by being an island inside East Germany, with the city itself being divided by the wall from 1961 to 1989. After the October 3, 1990, reunification, there was massive investment in what had been East Germany and East Berlin, with the result that newer buildings were of a different architectural species than in, say, Paris or much of London.

There remained in the city other evidence of its past. This included wonderful museums, Checkpoint Charlie, the Brandenburg Gate, and remnants of the Berlin Wall, which stirred the memories of those old enough to remember President Reagan saying to Mikhail Gorbachev in 1987 in a speech at the Brandenburg Gate, "Tear down this wall." And there were a number of thoughtful memorials demonstrating a deep national awareness of the Holocaust.

Louise and Salt found the Novatel hotel, near the Foreign Office, and checked in and grabbed some lunch while waiting for Gretchen. During 2000, the Foreign Office had moved from Bonn, the capital of West Germany before the reunification. Their meeting on Friday morning was going to be at the Federal Foreign Office, housed in a modern building at Werderscher Market, not far from the Spree River in an area of Berlin that housed a number of museums and government buildings.

Salt and Louise waited in the coffee shop for Gretchen Grant to arrive. She had landed in Berlin that morning on a typically delayed commercial red-eye flight from DC, waited forever on checked luggage, and then took a short nap when she arrived at the hotel. "How about a backgrounder on Gretchen?" Salt asked Louise while they were waiting.

"Top-notch," Louise said. "She will never carry a weapon in the field, but she can use her considerable people skills in almost any situation. She speaks two or three languages, has good judgment, and knows everyone in the Agency and at State. She's always in demand. And she's a nice person to boot."

"But can she spot tails?" asked Stuart, only half kidding.

"Sure, and she could track you without any difficulty," said Louise.

"That works for me," said Salt. "I guess I have to give Stuart credit. He's given me the all-stars to work with. He must think I need good help, and he would be right."

Gretchen joined them at 3:00 p.m. She was a bit taller and heavier than Louise, less athletic looking, had very curly, longish, dark hair, and was attractive. It took only sixty seconds to figure out that she was very smart, and German was one of her languages. They had a coffee in a quiet corner of the coffee shop and then adjourned to Salt's room for a more detailed chat and update.

"Well," said Salt, "this should be interesting. This will be a much different meeting than what we had in London. In this case, the Iranians contacted the Germans in an apparent effort to open things up. That means that Roland Theis, the federal minister for foreign affairs, is aware and will be involved at some level. At a minimum, we will be outranked. We can be sure that Stuart has spoken with the minister. I expect the minister to show up at some point in these meetings. We are to ask for a Martin Weber, who seems to be a troubleshooter of sorts for the minister and was involved in the JPCOA negotiations."

"I know him," said Gretchen. "He was involved on the fringes of the JCPOA and is smart and a bit hard to take. He's very linear in his thinking and will want to take the lead. I suggest we listen for the most part, express our willingness to play ball, talk about next steps, and let Stuart or the president arm wrestle with Martin and the minister about who takes the lead on this. My understanding is that Walter Williams will join us by phone tomorrow and remind us of the background so we can be sure we're all singing from the same hymnal.

"And by the way," Gretchen said, "word is that by the end of the day today in the United States, the president will send to the Senate Stuart Bacon's nomination to be secretary of state."

Salt said, "Shit. I knew this was coming but was not aware of the timing. It's critical that Stuart have a senior role in the new administration, but in the short run, he'll be diverted by preparing for Senate confirmation hearings and very hard to get hold of. We need to remember that, net, net, Stuart's nomination is a good thing over the long haul. We'll just have to put up with logistical issues in the short run, and there will be a higher risk of leaks associated this this project. Nothing is simple."

Gretchen gave to each of Salt and Louise copies of the detailed background briefing package that had been promised. "Something to keep you from being bored this evening before we meet with the Germans tomorrow morning," she said. They agreed that Gretchen would take it easy for the evening and that Salt and Louise would each have room service and study the briefing packages Gretchen had hauled over on the plane in her carry-on baggage.

CHAPTER TWENTY-EIGHT

Iranian Backgrounder II

They met for coffee on Friday morning and then headed for the Foreign Office. On the way over, Louise told Gretchen about the possibility of tails. "Interesting," commented Gretchen.

They were greeted at the Foreign Office by Martin Weber, who took their temperatures, provided masks, and escorted them to an interior and very modern conference room with no windows, gray walls, white counters, and glass tables. Nothing on the walls. The room felt cold and sterile, but any room that modern had to be very secure. Weber introduced three other members of the German team, two men and a woman, and said that Foreign Minister Theis would likely briefly join later.

Salt introduced Walter Williams, who had joined by secure land line from Washington, where it was the middle of the night. Salt explained that he wasn't sure who had arranged for Walter to join the session, but all agreed that it was a good idea to make sure the group had in mind a common set of background facts. Salt asked Walter to provide the *Reader's Digest* condensed version. If was, after all, Friday in Berlin, and there would be limits on attention spans.

Walter gave an overview of his background and reminded them that the Joint Comprehensive Plan of Action, or the JCPOA (what most people call the "Iran nuclear deal"), was signed in July 2015 after nearly two years of negotiations. The parties were Iran and the five permanent members of the UN Security Council (China, France, Russia, the UK, and the United States), plus Germany and the European Union. The agreement was preceded by years of smaller group negotiations, starting in 2003. The United States refused to participate in those discussions.

Walter continued, "The agreement was not perfect, as President Pope used to make clear. But in many respects, it was remarkable. Just getting those parties together and in agreement on anything for a term of fifteen years was a minor miracle."

"The treaty covered—and we gave Gretchen some written background on this to share with you: (1) nuclear capability, including inventory of enriched uranium and centrifuges and inspections by the International Atomic Energy Agency; (2) early stage exemptions from the nuclear provisions that allowed for the loosening of certain economic sanctions; and (3) broader relief from economic sanctions over time.

"The JCPOA was controversial in the United States at the time of and following adoption in 2015. The Obama administration was supportive of the agreement, but President Pope campaigned against the agreement in the 2016 presidential election. As you know, President Evans was a supporter of the principles behind the agreement during the negotiations and the 2020 campaign but didn't endorse the agreement as such."

Martin asked pointedly, "Can you please remind us of when the United States dropped out of the treaty?"

Walter answered, "President Pope withdrew from the agreement on May 8, 2018, and at the same time imposed harsher economic sanctions on Iran. The withdrawal was as controversial as entering into the agreement in the first place. Our understanding is that US allies were at first dumbfounded, then mad as hell. The other parties tried to hold the agreement together, but it fell into disrepair, pending the outcome of the US 2020 election. The difficulty of reinstating the treaty was also heightened by Iran's involvement in various hostilities in Iraq, Syria, Yemen, and Lebanon during 2020, and by the COVID-19 pandemic. And of course the status of the treaty is affected by geopolitical developments involving the United States, Russia, and China. This subject is a very complicated web."

Salt noted to himself that Walter was doing a nice job of providing a balanced recounting of the relevant history. There was very little pro-American bending of the facts. That was important for developing some credibility. The Germans recognized the same thing and did not present unbalanced questions or comments. The repartee was very civil.

Walter continued, "The current state of play is that, as a practical matter, the treaty is dead. There are a number of parties who want the agreement to be improved and brought back to life. But that won't happen without a strong signal of serious interest by the United States and Iran. Given the challenges associated with the United States, China, and Russia at the present time, the initial feeling is that it makes more sense for the United States and Iran and perhaps Germany to talk among themselves and make progress before bringing together a collection of other parties to the table, which at the present time would sort of resemble the bar scene in the first *Star Wars* movie. As evidenced by the initial contact here, of the non-US parties to the deal, Germany could probably be the most helpful. But we need to keep in mind that the Russians and Iranians are in constant dialogue."

Walter concluded, "So, that is the JCPOA for smart people, as opposed to dummies. A full briefing would take days, and we don't have days. And we frankly doubt that you need to be prepared for substantive discussions."

The group in Germany collectively thanked Walter, who then signed off. They took a break for the lunch of salads, small sandwiches, and crisps that had been brought in. All things considered, the mood was surprisingly relaxed. Salt wondered if the Germans were having a hard time taking this seriously.

During lunch, Martin Weber recommended that, at any meeting held during the next week to ten days, there should be no reason to try to make substantive progress. The agenda would be whether the

United States and Iran were serious about talking, who should be involved, and the logistics associated with what would need to be secret negotiations if at all possible.

Louise commented, "It feels to me like there's a one-day get-acquainted session with enough substance that we can get a useful sounding on the level of Iran's interest in meaningful discussions."

Others agreed with that shorthand overview.

CHAPTER TWENTY-NINE

German Minister Cameo

After lunch, Martin asked the American team, "Where do you think we go from here?" At that moment, Foreign Minister Roland Theis walked in and joined the meeting. "Perfect timing," said Martin, "as we were just starting to talk about what we want to do with this opportunity—if it is in fact an opportunity."

Salt suggested that it would be helpful to discuss again exactly what the Iranians had said to Martin and his team when they recently inquired about resuming discussions. "That's fair," said Minister Theis in perfect English, "but before we get into that, who are you, Salt? I've been banging around the diplomatic world for quite a while, and I've never run into you, and, no offense, you suddenly appear out of nowhere on behalf of President Evans and Stuart Bacon, talking about some very important stuff."

"Sorry, I thought Stuart had given you a backgrounder," replied Salt.

"He did," responded Minister Theis, "but you know Stuart; he tends to move through things quickly on a once-over-lightly basis."

"Well," said Salt, "I'm actually not the most qualified person for what I'm doing here, and I might not be qualified at all, but that's also the reason I'm here. Nobody in the world would guess that I'm up to serious diplomatic stuff, and nobody will confuse me with a decision maker. The likelihood of the media or others thinking I'm doing something newsworthy is low. I guess in some respects I'm the personification of expectations management. But I'm supported by two great emerging diplomats, Louise and Gretchen, as well as Walter, and I'm smart enough not to commit diplomatic suicide. I know that my foot does not belong in my mouth. And I'm not here because I made large political contributions to anyone. I'm essentially apolitical but committed to finding the middle ground in nearly all of what I do. There can't be an excessive number of winners and losers in what we do—an approach the last US administration rejected."

Salt went on to provide a bit more background on his career at Treasury, State, and the law firm. Minister Theis and the others listened intently.

Salt continued, "I may as well be completely candid about our mission here. When we left the United States early this week, we were to visit with close allies, including Germany, about how we could repair and enhance diplomatic relations with key allies and others around the world. Germany was at the top of the list, and we want and need to talk with you about Germany, the EU and the region more generally, and global health issues. But you folks received the call from Iran, and we had to divert. That does not mean we're not vitally interested in the Germany-Europe discussions. Indeed, we would characterize those topics as both urgent and important."

When Salt was done, the minister said, "Well, thanks for that last bit. It helps provide context for how you were pulled into these discussions. You're an unconventional choice for all of this, but you are on an unconventional mission. So maybe you are perfect. Just please keep in mind that Germany's credibility is also at stake in this enterprise, and it must be said that our reaction to you is tainted by our experience with your last administration. To be candid, we have been double-crossed by the United States too often; we will be careful here. The lack of trust is palpable throughout Germany. Not only will our diplomats be concerned about collaboration with the United States, so will the general public. We must not be seen as being very committed to anything. Please understand that this is not personal—at least not yet." And only then did Minister Theis smile.

"I get it," said Salt. "And I appreciate your candor. We may actually be able to get along."

"Good," said Minister Theis. "You may speak with Martin as if you were talking to me, and I expect him to keep me fully up to date. Carry on." And he left.

Salt was not sure what to make of the discussion with the minister, who seemed like a reasonable guy and was surprisingly direct and informal. It was clear that the minister did not want to have his fingerprints on this escapade, and he felt strongly enough about that to cede control to someone who probably should not be in the lead. The posture of things could not be better for the Germans. If things headed south, they had both plausible deniability and someone to blame. *No guts, no glory*, thought Salt.

CHAPTER THIRTY

Berlin: Next Steps

Salt pretended that he had not sorted things out in his own mind. "Damn," he said. "We didn't get into next steps with the minister before he left."

"Right," said Martin. "There are two reasons for that. First, he thinks you might be okay, if a strange choice. For now, you get the benefit of the doubt. Second, in any event, he wants personal plausible deniability. You have just finished an election in the United States. Here we are facing one. And it's very hard to guess as to the fate of our chancellor, what a new coalition government might look like, where the minister might fit in, and the effect of all of this on the stability of Europe. So, bottom line, as you Americans say, we are both a little bit at loose ends in terms of oversight. We had best not screw things up."

With that, they took a fifteen-minute break, with each team going to its corner of the large room. Salt explained his situational analysis, and the others concurred. Like it or not, the US contingent was going to lead the meeting with Iran.

They resumed with Martin returning to the question of what happens next, and Salt returning to the question of what the Iranians had said.

"Okay," said Martin, "I'll go first. I was in the room, and they said very little. There were only two of them. They said that, with the change of US administrations, it seemed like a logical moment to consider resuming discussions, but they had not had much comfortable contact with the new US administration. Since they know some of us, they decided to ask for our thoughts." Martin reviewed some of the dialogue from the meeting. The Germans asked if the Iranians had any proposals, especially on the nuclear issues. The answer was no. The Germans also asked what would be the Iranian goals for any discussions, and the answer was speedy relief from economic sanctions, which were creating domestic instability and making worse the dire COVID-19 conditions. The German team responded that talking about sanctions relief without nuclear issues being on the table was a nonstarter. At a minimum, there would need to be simultaneous progress, and the Germans said the allies and other parties might require progress on nuclear issues before any relief could be had. The Iranians expressed disappointment with that news, but in truth, they knew that would be the answer.

"In other words," concluded Salt, "on the surface, the meeting was a waste of time, but it was still a signal that Iran has domestic unrest issues over the effects of sanctions and the coronavirus and wants to be in a room with us."

"That's a bit oversimplified, but right," said Martin.

Louise observed, "What this means is that a first meeting involving the United States is necessary but will end up being a nothing sandwich. And realistically, we will not have any proposals to table. This feels like we will be wasting time and money on another exercise that is probably something we need to do but hard to get excited about in a positive way."

Gretchen asked, "Are we saying that we're willing to have a meeting so long as we don't offer or give up anything and use it to try to smoke out some further information from them?"

"I think so," said Salt. "What's your take, Martin?"

Martin stated, "We are in agreement, but I need to try to catch the minister before he leaves. Why don't we leave the conference room for an hour so you can try to reach the United States, and we'll touch base with the minister. By the way, what would we propose for a meeting place? Berlin? Vienna? Geneva?"

Salt thought for a few moments. "Those are all fine, but they're venues where serious discussions have taken place. I'm not sure we're ready for a prime-time location where we might be noticed by a very sophisticated press. I would try Prague. It's a great city and lower profile than the others. If we get a meeting arranged, I would try to get use of a meeting room in the Zofin Palace on the river just south of the Old Town area in Prague."

"Works for me," said Martin. "We'll check back with you in an hour."

Since she was more of a regular at State, Gretchen made the calls to try to catch up with Stuart in the United States. Calls to his shoe phone were not answered, which wasn't a surprise, and they had no idea who Stuart was closeted with, though most likely it involved the Senate confirmation process. They called Walter, brought him up to date, and asked him to try to find Stuart and get a green light.

After reconvening, they advised Martin of the state of play with Stuart, and Martin had good news—Minister Theis was okay with the plan with several conditions. First, it had to stay secret. If at any time the cover was blown, the Germans would cease talking and deny that there had been any recent conversations. Second, he wanted a formulation of the allies' position on uranium enrichment that could be used as vague teaser with the Iranians, but it had to be a hard ask. Finally, before going into serious discussions, it would be necessary to get back relevant hostages. The team needed to identify what that meant.

The teams agreed to caucus among themselves around these assignments on Saturday and meet again on Sunday at one in the afternoon to understand status, build talking points, and be prepared for a meeting with the Iranians as early as possible in the next week. Since he had been involved in the last discussions with the Iranians, it was agreed that the US team would ask Martin to make the call to suggest a meeting during the next week. Those with assignments went off to attend to them.

Thirty minutes later, Martin opened a panel on one wall of the conference room that hid a bar, and they went informal on bar snacks, spirits, and German beer. Later, Gretchen, Louise, and Salt agreed to have a nonbusiness dinner and meet at one o'clock on Saturday afternoon to formulate ideas for discussions with their new German friends on Sunday afternoon—unless things got shot down (literally or figuratively) in the meantime.

Berlin was hopping that Friday night, not paying much attention to social distancing and masks, and the US team had to wait for a table in a trendy restaurant, but they survived and enjoyed the seafood. Salt thought, *This is not Carterville.*

They went to their rooms immediately after getting back to the hotel. That evening, after getting ready to go to bed, Salt shaved and then knocked on Louise's door down the hallway. She welcomed him in. Once again, nothing was said.

CHAPTER THIRTY-ONE

Berlin: Game Plan Emerges

Saturday was a busy day but not as crammed as the prior week had been. Salt worked out and took a walk, Louise did a serious workout and run, and Gretchen caught up on other things that had been on her plate before being volunteered for this unusual gig.

The team gathered at one o'clock in Salt's room and discussed overall state of play and approaches to the meeting with the Iranians. Being the new player on the team, Gretchen led off and commented that the minister did not even attempt to hide his view that the US players were an unconventional and motley crew, and of course it was hard to disagree with that assessment. Salt was pleased that the interaction among the US team members was healthy and without the hierarchy so common in such efforts. Gretchen and Louise were straightforward, noting for Salt's sake that they—more than Salt—would need to be careful and duck when the blame started to be thrown around, as it almost certainly would.

During the discussion, Martin called and said he had spoken with the Iranians and there was tentative agreement on a very clandestine meeting in Prague on the following Wednesday.

To some extent, there was nothing to prepare for, as nothing would be agreed to. This was going to be a preliminary meeting to a preliminary meeting. The key thing was to listen so as to be able to unpack what was being communicated rather than being distracted by what was said.

Key parameters to the discussion had to include (1) the hostage point made by Minister Theis, (2) Iran ceasing entirely an increasing level of cyberwarfare, (3) reinstatement of nuclear provisions with clear milestones that were a bit tougher than in the JCPOA and also at least as verifiable as the measures included in the first deal, (4) a lifting of sanctions that would take place over time and could not be characterized as a giveaway, (5) cessation of terrorist support by Iran, and (6) some emergency COVID-19 assistance to Iran. None of this would be easy. This was particularly true as to nuclear capability, as it had become clear that Iran had exceeded the level of enriched uranium allowed by the JCPOA by early 2020. This wasn't a case of stopping enrichment at a current level but rather retreating from the current state of play.

They developed their outline, put it an email with the bullet points to be reviewed by Walter and Stuart before sharing with the Germans, and then hit send. Walter reacted with a few comments later in the day.

Before breaking up, they discussed among themselves whether Salt and Louise had been tailed. Louise was firm in her belief that they had been tailed in London, and her educated guess was that the tails were Russian. Neither Salt nor Gretchen had a good reason to disagree. It could have been almost anyone, including the Germans, Iraqis, Turks, or Iranians. Whoever it was, they were good. The likelihood of an incident seemed low, but if and when it became apparent that the US team would be in discussions with the Iranians, the interest level would change dramatically.

CHAPTER THIRTY-TWO

Berlin: Straight Talk

Gretchen had made arrangements to catch up with an old friend for dinner on Sunday. That left Louise and Salt to fend for themselves. This had the potential to be awkward. Louise asked shyly, "Do you have other plans or want to be alone, or would you like to have dinner together?"

"If you don't have other plans, I have had more than enough dinners with myself over the years. Let's have the concierge try to find us a place that's relatively quiet and nearby, with quiet being more important than nearby," suggested Salt.

"Good," said Louise. "Why don't you deal with the concierge, pick someplace, and just let me know what time and if there's a dress code."

"Done."

They met in the lobby at six thirty. Earlier in the day, Salt had had on jeans, but he was in a sport coat and trousers now. Louise had been in workout clothes earlier in the day and had not changed into one of her black pantsuits. She was still in a pantsuit but much different looking than the black versions. Salt wondered what her secret was in terms of packing.

They got to the restaurant, ordered a bottle of reasonable red, and waited for each other to break the silence.

"Okay," said Salt, "I'll go first." He spoke quietly and carefully. "I'm sorry and disappointed in myself that I may have taken advantage of you on this trip. I have never done anything like that before, and it won't happen again. I never cheated on my wife while traveling—or otherwise—and I'm not a one-night stand kind of guy. And that includes with women who are almost young enough to be my daughter. You're smart, very pretty even when wearing a black pantsuit, and apparently not in a relationship, so you're very attractive in all kinds of ways. You need to be careful as well. We may need to report this to someone in the chain of command so they can get rid of me, though I'm technically a consultant who can be fired at any moment in time. If you're uncomfortable, I'll leave Berlin now and report why to Stuart. If you can stand it, I think that should wait for a few days so we can get this first Iranian meeting behind us. I can then disappear without any awkwardness."

"Shhhheeesh," Louise responded in a heated tone. "First, I can take care of myself. If you were stupid enough to try to force me into something—and I know you would never do that—you would end up needing medical care. I have skills you have not yet seen. Get over that. Second, I think I was the first violator here, and I'm sorry about that—or maybe not. Third, although I try not to look it, my age starts with a five. Fourth, my guess is that until a few days ago, neither of us had slept with a member of the opposite sex for nearly a year. That's not good. Finally, you are a Boy Scout—as I have said before—but there is nothing inherently wrong with Boy Scouts. You know the Boy Scout motto is *be prepared*. That's good advice for dealing with me. And the first time I crawled in bed with you, you were prepared.

"Look," she continued, "I'm not suggesting that I'm falling in love with you or anything like that—who knows how you deal with that—but I think I could enjoy your company outside of working together, especially if you got used to black pantsuits for me and better ties for yourself. And God knows we could use some stress relief. My suggestion is that we not get hung up on this, or impose on each other, or let whatever it is we have interfere at all with the mission. In other words, let's see how this develops and in the meantime get over it."

"That sounds like a great resolution for the time being." Salt smiled. "Thanks."

"See?" said Louise. "You actually can smile."

They went on to enjoy a good dinner and a discussion about things other than the mission. When they got back to the hotel, it was awkward. They were silent in the elevator and while walking to their rooms. Louise finally said as she got to her door, "You have ten minutes to knock on my door. After that, I'm going to sleep."

Salt knocked.

CHAPTER THIRTY-THREE

On to Prague

On Sunday after coffee, working out, more coffee, and breakfast, the US team got together and walked over to the German Foreign Office.

"There it is again," said Louise.

"What?" asked Gretchen.

"The feeling that we're being watched," responded Louise. "I wonder if Tweedledee and Tweedledum are back with us."

Nobody was stupid enough to stop and look, but the group picked up the pace more or less automatically. As they walked over to the German Foreign Office, Salt commented that even he felt it now, and that his guess was that they were Russians or someone working for the Russians. He wondered out loud what had tipped them off, but maybe it was just standard operating procedure, as Peter Banks had suggested in London. In any event, there were no incidents on the walk over.

Martin Weber let them in and guided them to the same conference room they had been in on Friday. "Welcome again," said Martin, "and thanks for your suggestions. We have spoken with Minister Theis, and he is satisfied with the overall direction. It must be said, however, that he is not optimistic about anything coming of this. Frankly, if he thought this initiative—or even this meeting—was going to have any positive results, he might have wanted to lead the mission himself. In that connection, and no offense intended, he is a bit concerned that we are sending to this first meeting people who do not have enough stature, such that there is a risk that the Iranians will be offended."

Salt said, "Well, we were pretty transparent about that with you and Minister Theis, as well as with Stuart, when we said we had similar concerns, but there is also the significant risk of this getting into the media if any outsiders notice and take the initiative seriously. Gretchen will try to reach Stuart and run this by him once more, but I doubt there will be a change in the game plan."

"Fine," responded Martin. "In that case, we're glad for you to be the primary spokesperson, Salt." Salt smiled, as he felt a little like the donkey in a pin the tail on the donkey game, but there was nothing to be gained by further debate over whether this would work at all.

They turned to the working draft of the bullet points that outlined the messages to be delivered but not handed out. None of them would be easy. The US-German team would acknowledge a need to continue to ease some sanctions and provide some COVID-19 relief, but they were not willing to follow the course of action followed by President Pope in dealing with North Korea. There needed to be actual verifiable progress on the nuclear side of things before there would be material sanctions movement. Or—since it might be easier and demonstrate mutual good faith—there could be some minor measure of relief in the event of hostage releases or a verified reduction of sponsored terrorist activity. Getting out of the cyberwarfare business would also have value. And, recognizing the serious nature of the impact of sanctions, the allies would be willing to move the talks along quickly.

After a couple hours of discussion, they decided there was nothing further to game play, and they broke up.

As they were walking out of the Foreign Office, Salt asked Gretchen to try to track down Stuart or, if he wasn't responding, Walter, who might be able to reach Stuart, and tell Stuart again that the Germans were not happy with the greenhorn nature of the team, especially Salt.

On the way back to the hotel, they had the same feeling about being tailed. Salt laughed quietly and suggested, a bit tongue in cheek, that the CIA might be following them. All agreed that anything was possible as they made dinner plans.

After dinner, when they were back at the hotel and Gretchen had gotten off the elevator at a lower floor, Salt said to Louise, "I doubt I'm in a position to meet later. I have a text from Stuart saying that he wants to talk to me this evening and will call sometime in the next hour or so."

Louise said, "Hmm, that should be interesting. Good luck and get some rest. Text me a quick summary when you're done with the call."

A few minutes later, after Salt was settled in his room, his shoe phone rang. It was Stuart. "Walter has brought me up to date, including the disparaging comments by Theis. He needs to get over it, but more important, so do you. Do not—repeat *do not*—continue suggesting that you are not the right guy for this. You are there on the ground and need to take charge. You're the right guy for two reasons. You are in fact a right guy. And you have been sold as a right guy. We all know you don't care about your neck. But my neck is out there on this, and so are Louise's and Gretchen's. Use your Monday to clear your head and do something like go to a couple of the great museums there in Berlin. And get yourself to Prague early so there's no hassle."

Stuart seemingly spoke without taking a breath, and it was clear that Salt was to listen and not talk very much, if at all. Stuart also explained that, although it was not certain that one would be needed (Louise spoke Arabic), State was sending from Baghdad an interpreter for the meeting. Salt and the team should brief her or him.

"Okay—I get the message," said Salt. "We can talk about longer term after this week. By the way, has anyone mentioned to you these two guys who may have been tailing us in London and here in Berlin?"

"Yeah," responded Stuart. "If you're being tailed, it's not us. Maybe we need to think about giving you some protection, but that wouldn't be very low profile. We've told Louise to be careful and ready. Everyone in the world is trying to figure out our new foreign policy; it's not surprising that someone would be curious as to what you're up to. It may be nothing, but you can't be too careful these days. Good luck." Stuart hung up.

Salt texted Louise, "No change in plans," and then texted both Louise and Gretchen about working out in the morning before breakfast, having someone get them on a flight to Prague on Monday night or early Tuesday, rooms at the Hilton near Old Town in Prague for them and the interpreter, and getting together with the interpreter in Prague on Tuesday. For once, he was able to go to sleep quickly.

Monday was actually relaxing. Salt briefed Gretchen and Louise about his listening session with Stuart during breakfast. By midmorning, they were booked on an evening flight to Prague and ready to burn some time museum hopping and shopping. It was a break they all needed.

The flight to Prague was uneventful, as was the short cab ride into downtown. In the cab, Salt explained to Louise and Gretchen that Prague was one of his favorite cities in the world. Prague had avoided much damage during World War II and while part of the Soviet bloc, and had a lovely Old Town area, complete with a wonderful town square and an amazing astronomical clock dating from the 1550s. The Charles Bridge crossed the river near Old Town, and on the opposite side of the river, the foot traffic followed a pedestrian street that led up a hill to a medieval castle. Salt once had a colleague who had traveled a great deal and described Prague as the "best museum-quality city" in Europe. Salt agreed. If one had to be someplace in Europe, Prague was a good place to be—even though it was plenty cold in early February.

CHAPTER THIRTY-FOUR

Facing the Iranian Front

Tuesday was a relaxing day in terms of meetings. But Salt was on edge, constantly playing though his mind possible scenarios for the meeting with the Iranians. It was good that he didn't have to concentrate on anything else. He expected that the other members of the team were similarly distracted, but they were leaving him alone. The weather wasn't too bad, so they got together in the middle of the afternoon and walked through Old Town, browsed in a couple of the crystal shops, and hiked across the Charles Bridge and up to the castle and back. They noted that seemingly everyone was wearing a mask. There was no sign of Tweedledee and Tweedledum. But they could be en route.

The group caught up late in the afternoon with the interpreter, who turned out to be a UK citizen whose family had moved from Baghdad before Iraq invaded Kuwait and was thoroughly English. She was smart and would be very good if needed.

They had arranged for a private room in the hotel for dinner with the small German team, consisting of Martin Weber and two others. They had considered getting a room in the US or German embassy for dinner, but that could have been a low-profile breaker.

The dinner discussion did not add anything of substance. They seemed to be as ready as they could be.

The meeting on the following morning was at the Zofin Palace, which was built in 1836–37 and was an amazing neo-renaissance building on an island in the Vltava River just south of Old Town. It was now owned by the city of Prague. It was quite lovely both inside and out but not what one would call a tourist attraction. It was used for cultural events and as a conference center. The US team had arranged for the use of an obscure but very classy conference room on the mezzanine level with a view of the river.

The US and German teams walked from the hotel to the meeting and arrived around 10:15 a.m. The Iranian team, consisting of three members plus an interpreter, arrived promptly at 10:30 a.m. The leader of the Iranian team was Ashkan Gilani. The Germans knew a bit about him from previous discussions and had given Salt a heads-up that Gilani could show up at the meeting. Gretchen had also done some homework on him. Gilani was low profile in Iran but would not have been selected if the leadership of Iran did not trust him.

After donning their masks and engaging in the mandatory introductions and pleasantries, the teams sat down in a socially distanced pattern for discussions. Gilani spoke first. "Our team is fluent in English, and I assume the German team is as well. Therefore, I propose to hold the meeting in English, with help from the interpreters as needed."

"Agreed," said Salt.

Gilani continued, "Before we start, we have one question. No offense intended, but who are you, Mr. Pepper? We have no record of you being in prior meetings with either Iranians or Iraqis, and we need to understand your role here."

Keeping in mind Stuart's admonition from the Monday-night call, Salt responded, "Surely you do not think the United States would send to a meeting like this someone the new administration does not have confidence in. At least to some extent, you asked for this meeting because there is a new US administration. In that context, you should expect to see new people. That does not mean they are ignorant or not empowered. However, we accept your question as being well intentioned, if slightly insulting. The answer to your question is that I am a duly authorized representative of the United States with authority to speak on behalf of secretary of state designate Stuart Bacon."

"Thank you," said Gilani. "As I said, we meant no offense. You must understand that we have to wonder if you are a new version of, or how you compare to, the last president's so-called personal lawyer, Mr. Rubin."

Salt smiled. "I'll have to give you points on that one, Ashkan. But I will readily admit that I don't compare to Mr. Rubin."

Gilani clearly understood both the obvious and nonobvious content of that reply. He continued, "Well, if you have questions about our bona fides, we are glad to answer your questions."

"Thanks," said Salt, "but that is not necessary, as we have done our homework before arriving. And we understand that while our governments in the United States and Germany may be in various stages of transition, yours may be as well."

That jab resulted in the silent treatment for a few moments, with members of the Iranian delegation looking at one another with raised eyebrows.

Salt decided to break the ice: "Your government asked for this meeting. Perhaps it would be helpful for you to explain why."

"It is really quite simple," responded Gilani. "The current state of relations between Iran, on the one hand, and the United States and its allies, on the other, is not a basis for peace. We agreed to a comprehensive treaty in 2015 only to have, shall we say, an impulsive US president unilaterally drop out of the agreement at a time when all concerned agree that Iran was in compliance with its obligations under what you call the JCPOA. This was a massive insult to all of the parties involved and especially to Iran. It is understandable, therefore, that Iran has backed away from the JCPOA, and unless it can be fixed, we will ignore it."

Salt responded, "Look, we know that you have already backed away from the 2015 agreement, as you are well above the JCPOA enriched uranium limits as we sit here today, perhaps by a factor of

10. And we are aware of the explosions that took place in some of your nuclear facilities last July."

"Perhaps," said Gilani. "You also know that we could have taken much more aggressive actions in response to US provocations, but decided not to do so before understanding more about the US attitude and plan."

Then Gilani sat back and said in perfect, unaccented English, "Look—we do not understand much about you or the new administration. But we can't wait long for progress in the US-Europe-Iran relationship. And we cannot engage in substantive discussions at all until we have meaningful relief from the ridiculous economic sanctions the United States has in place against Iran and its leading citizens. Truly, if there is a weapon of mass destruction that has been detonated, it is the US sanctions. They have caused severe and unwarranted harm to Iranian citizens, especially with the effects of COVID-19. You know from your satellite surveillance that we are digging trenches to serve as graves for the poor souls who die from the disease. You need to understand the seriousness of the situation. It is criminal. America must also call off its Israeli dogs who regularly bomb our people and sabotage our facilities."

Salt was quiet for a moment and then responded. "We designed the sanctions to work well and have effects proportionate to the actions of Iran vis-à-vis Iraq, nuclear capabilities, terrorist support, cybercrime, and other issues of concern. Our satellite surveillance also shows that Iran is active in Syria, Yemen, and Iraq. You complain about Israel and refer to us as criminals while you create an incredible level of despair in places like Syria, Lebanon and Yemen. The whole world knows what you are up to in Venezuela. And as you know, we made humanitarian exceptions to the sanctions in relation to COVID-19. I'm a person who searches for the middle ground, but there can be no discussion of sanctions relief without material progress on these related issues. That is the substantive position of the United States because it is right, and you also need to understand the US political limitations on what it can agree to. The new administration will not follow here the North Korea discussion model embraced by the prior administration."

Gilani frowned. "Perhaps we need to meet separately in the room next door to discuss things among ourselves. Do you assure me that there are no listening devices in that room?"

Salt responded, "I'm sure it is wired for something, but we're not a party to that and have no listening capability in that room. And the national government of the Czech Republic does not know we are here."

With that, the teams separated for discussions among themselves that ended up going through the consumption of sandwiches that arrived during those discussions.

They reconvened at 1:00 p.m. Gilani opened. "We may be at an impasse for today. We have told you that we need up-front sanctions relief before we can participate in substantive discussions. Could you please give us an overview of what you need if we are to achieve that?"

Salt responded without hesitating. "Certainly, and not necessarily in priority order: (1) release of all hostages with ties to the parties to the JCPOA; (2) cessation of sponsored cyberattacks; (3) reinstatement of nuclear limitations with a longer term, lower levels of enriched product than called for by the JCPOA, and higher levels of verifiability; and (4) cessation of support of terrorist organizations and activities."

Gilani reacted immediately: "But this is ridiculous. You walk away from a treaty and then demand that your position must be improved from what it was under the treaty in order to reinstate the treaty? And you dare to do that after depriving our people of help from the coronavirus. How typical of America."

"I'm sorry you feel that way, especially given the COVID-19 assistance we have provided," said Salt. "Perhaps we need to think about these issues and resume discussions at another time but soon."

"Well, in that case, we have found one thing we agree on today," Gilani responded as he packed his papers and then left with his team.

After the Iranians left, the Americans and the Germans took a few minutes to compare notes, with all agreeing that the meeting was about what should have been expected in a first meeting. Martin

Weber would report back to Minister Theis, and the Americans would report back to Stuart Bacon. The Germans would get on an evening flight to Berlin. The American team was stuck in Prague for the evening and would take a morning flight back to Washington with a connection through Frankfurt.

After the German team departed, the Americans spent time in the Palace conference room agreeing on the message to go back to Stuart. Basically, the results were not surprising, there was no real harm (or good) done, and next steps, if any, would depend on what the Iranians came back with.

The American team then packed their papers and started to walk along the river back to Old Town and the hotel. As they were walking, a young athletic male wearing a stocking cap and a mask ran up behind Louise and grabbed her bag with her papers in it. She knew immediately that she had a crisis on her hands; it would be a disaster if a foreign power got possession of her copious notes and other materials in her bag. Her black pantsuit wasn't an issue, but Louise did not have on the right shoes for a chase, though she took off like a bolt of lightning after the guy, pulling her pistol out of her small handbag as she ran. As she neared the guy, she started yelling at him, and the crowd on the sidewalk started to rush off the river side of the sidewalk and get out of the way. Louise started yelling in Arabic without success. She hollered again in English, and the guy didn't stop. Louise was losing a shoe and about to lose ground. Having no choice, she fired her pistol once into the air and hollered one more time, this time yelling, "Stohp!" with a Russian accent. Taking advantage of the parting of the crowd, Louise stopped and took aim. The guy must have seen Louise take aim. He wisely dropped the bag and took off. It was not clear whether the Russian "Stohp" or the pistol did the trick. But he didn't look back and kept going.

Louise picked up her bag, and the team hustled off into a crowded, narrow cobblestone side street and kept going. They were quickly lost in the crowd. They kept to themselves; the last thing they could do was draw attention to themselves or report something to the local police.

Back at the hotel, Louise confirmed that she had recovered all of her papers. They discussed whether this was a local hit, the work of the tails who had picked them up in London and Berlin, or someone new ordered in from Moscow or Tehran. Salt agreed with Louise that they maybe had more surveillance than they thought. And it could be that the Iranians had leaked the meeting, either purposely or inadvertently. They guy who grabbed Louise's bag was a new player; TweedleDee and Tweedledum were much more subtle and of a different persuasion.

Louise deposited her bag at the hotel desk to be put in the safe, Gretchen called and gave an update to Walter, who would in turn update Stuart, and the team headed out for another walk around Old Town, a stiff drink, and a decent dinner.

The next morning, Thursday, Gretchen attended to some sightseeing, and Salt and Louise took off on the long flight, connecting through Frankfurt, and arrived at Dulles International around 10:00 p.m. without incident. They were in coach again and were not able to talk much through their masks during the flight, but both had plenty to think about. They knew Stuart was occupied on Friday with Senate confirmation hearing preparation. They had tentatively scheduled a meeting with Stuart on Monday afternoon. Salt and Louise parted ways after landing. Salt found his car in the long-term parking lot at Dulles and headed for Carterville, with a plan to take Friday off. He and Louise would touch base sometime over the weekend.

CHAPTER THIRTY-FIVE

Back on the Farm

It was sort of good to be home, but Salt had to ask himself whether the farm was really home—and what was he going to do with all the damn moving boxes? They didn't seem to be disappearing on their own.

Salt slept in on Friday morning, found some instant coffee and very stale rolls that were inedible, took a shower, and made his short-term survival grocery list. Over his lousy cup of coffee, he began to think about what came next. He had been too tired on the plane back to the United States to think seriously about such things and had focused instead on watching a series of bad movies. It was hard work to try to think cogently about complex issues.

The issues included: (1) did Salt want to retire or not?; (2) if so, where?; (3) if not, what would he do?; (4) was Stuart interested in having him continue on something?; (5) if so, what?; (6) what about Louise?; and (7) what about Margie? This was complicated—lots of interdependent and moving pieces.

Salt thought about all of these issues but did not resolve any of them, in part because he was still in transition in terms of losing his wife and moving and retiring and so on, and he wasn't really aware of what Stuart had in mind for him. His first efforts had not had dazzling results; maybe Stuart was no longer relevant. Salt decided that he needed to continue to think about things and reassess as the number of uncertainties decreased. Or was that just an excuse for avoiding the whole can of worms?

Late in the morning, he went to the grocery and returned to the farm to make himself a ham sandwich for lunch. He then forced himself to work on more boxes for the rest of the afternoon. He made himself another ham sandwich for dinner, had a drink, watched a western movie that didn't make him think, and went to bed.

On Saturday, he slept in again, showered, and moved around a few more boxes, pretending that it represented meaningful progress. The coronavirus-shortened football season was over, and he wasn't a big fan of basketball on TV, so there was nothing on TV that represented a compelling diversion. Since he was bored and listless, he talked himself into needing to get his hair trimmed again. He called Georgie's and got a number.

He had some time to kill, so he called his tenant, Jack Davis, to see how things were going. It had only been a couple weeks since he last spoke with Jack. Salt just wanted to let Jack know he was interested. Jack answered the phone.

"Hi, Jack," Salt said. "I've been out of town and just thought I would check in. How are things going?"

"No news here," responded Jack. "I'm still thinking about what, if anything, to plant. Am I better off taking whatever the government will give me to leave the ground fallow, or should I plant something? You know, the biggest factor in the market is China. We're still waiting to see the end of the so-called China trade war that President Pope was going to resolve before he got distracted by the damn impeachment mess, and then both we and the Chinese had to focus on the massive coronavirus pandemic. Then our election took precedence. As a result, still nothing is resolved. Meanwhile, the farmers of America are feeling like pawns. President Evans needs to get a move on.

"Look, Salt," Jack said, "I have some grain in storage that I'll have to sell at some point. I don't know what to do or when. I'll need money if I decide to plant in the spring, but as I say, I don't know what to plant—or if. I hope you'll continue to be patient, and that someone in DC understands that a lot of us are hanging on by our fingernails."

"That's easy," said Salt. "Do what makes the most sense for you and your family, and we'll work things out when things start to move one way or another. Take care of yourself."

CHAPTER THIRTY-SIX

Georgie's: Progress toward the Middle

Salt did not really need a trim, but he did not feel like spending the entire day alone either. Besides, he was wondering if anything had come of his political football game. When Salt called and asked for a number, Georgie estimated that Salt's number would be called around 2:15 p.m., so Salt decided to be safe and head for Georgie's a bit early. When Salt walked into the shop, he noticed that the excess chairs were still stacked in the corner to allow for social distancing, and all of the barbers and most of the customers were wearing masks. All eyes were focused on the TV. "What's on?" asked Salt.

"You mean you don't know, pointy-head?" asked Georgie in his more sarcastic tone. "Hell, man, this is Atlantic Coast Conference—we call it ACC—basketball territory, and Virginia is playing North Carolina. Kindly get the hell out of my line of sight so I can watch the game out of the side of my eye without butchering my current customer. I need to multitask if I'm ever going to get to you."

"Okay, okay, sorry," responded Salt. "Who are you rooting for?"

"Anyone other than Duke and North Carolina, and at the top of the favorites list around here is Virginia," explained Georgie.

"You're a pretty big guy," commented Georgie. "Did you play basketball when you were in high school here?"

"Sort of," responded Salt. "I was on the team but didn't play much."

"Sorry," said Georgie, "but now I have to ask. How much is not much?"

"Little enough that one day when the coach was in a foul mood, he told me I should just stop practicing and do squats instead."

"What did that mean?" asked Georgie.

Salt smiled. "He was telling me in his own code that the only action I was going to see was getting up off the bench at time-outs and the end of quarters and then sitting back down, so I might as well do something relevant like squats."

Several in the barbershop stifled laughs.

"Don't worry," said Salt. "I'm over it and have to laugh at myself. By the way, how is my political football game going?"

"See for yourself," said Georgie. "Take down some of the new notices and see what your bulletin board looks like."

Salt did as instructed and was pleased with what he uncovered. True to the understanding, Georgie had handed out pushpins and asked customers to place a pin on the corkboard—as if it were an illustration of a football field—to represent the player's political views. Most of the pins were between the thirty-five-yard lines. There were a few in the extremes (what you might call the red zones or even the end zones), and a few, like Salt, were right on or very close to the fifty-yard line.

"We played honest," said Georgie. "We did not look when customers put their pins on the bulletin board—well not much anyhow—and we didn't give anyone shit about where they placed their pins. It was better than a news poll. No margin of error."

"That's right," commented Max, the other male barber. "We kept Georgie on the straight and narrow here. And you were right; most people are looking for middle ground and are not extremists."

"*Most* people," said Don, the retired guy / hunter / NRA member who Salt had met the first time he was in Georgie's shop, "would be the operative phrase. That's me in the right end zone, and proud to be there—and I'm not alone, you will notice."

"That's great," commented Salt. "The point of this exercise is that there is a wide spectrum of political views, and if you want to get anything done, you'll likely need a mix of support from both sides of the fifty-yard line. We don't have to agree on everything, but we should where there is common ground, as between, say, the thirty-five- or forty-yard lines."

"I'll admit that it was sort of interesting," said Georgie, "and Max and Ellen and I decided we would leave the bulletin board up for another couple of weeks before taking it down. But now the question is, what are your pointy-headed friends going to do with all of this postelection goodwill? Best they not piss it away."

"I would be very surprised if they didn't understand that," said Salt, hoping to himself that the new administration could deliver.

Georgie finished with his customer and said to Salt, "Okay, you're up. Ready to lower your ears."

"I just need a trim," said Salt. "I'm not sure, but I may be going on a business trip and thought I should get less shaggy in case I need to go. Besides, I wanted to see whether you had destroyed the political football game."

As Georgie was finishing up, Salt said, "So now that I'm a regular here, do I qualify for the Hair-i-Care program?"

"Well, we have a new application form," said Georgie. "Take a look while I'm finishing your trim." Georgie handed Salt the new form, which included the following questions:

Hair-i-Care Application

Name: _____

1. Are you a woman or a male with black or brown skin? If so, stop here. You qualify.
2. Are you seventy or older?

> 3. Have you had five of your last six haircuts here?
> 4. Did you participate in our political football game?
> 5. Have you volunteered anywhere during the past two months?
> 6. If you are a male and you used our restroom for #1, did you lift the seat?
> 7. And then was your aim good so you hit the hole?
> 8. Did you vote in the recent presidential election?
> 9. What was the name of the American poet who scratched the following poem on the back of a pay toilet stall door in a Pennsylvania Turnpike restroom in the 1950s: "Here I sit all broken hearted, paid a dime to crap and only farted"?

"Well, I guess I don't qualify," said Salt.

"Right," said Georgie, "but keep working on it. Someday you'll get there."

"How many do you have to get right?" Salt asked.

"Depends," said Georgie.

"On what?" asked Salt.

"A lot of things," said Georgie, "including what kind of mood I'm in. So stop acting like one of those liberal media reporters on cable news always asking way too many stupid questions."

"Got it," said Salt. He shut up. The ACC basketball game was over, leaving most in a bad mood since North Carolina had overcome a stingy Virginia defense and won. The shop began to empty out about the same time Georgie was done with Salt. As he was leaving, Salt asked for a hint on item eight of the Hair-i-Care questions.

"No way," responded Georgie. "You're a pointy-headed member of the Deep State from Washington, DC; you are a primo leak risk."

Salt smiled, paid Georgie, and left.

CHAPTER THIRTY-SEVEN

Suits Salt

Having talked to Jack Davis, been to the grocery, had his haircut, and not being eager to return to a lonely and messy farmhouse, Salt decided to take a chance and call Margie Hatcher. She answered the phone, and Salt explained that he had been unexpectedly out of town and felt he owed her a call. He screwed up his courage and asked if she had time for dinner on Sunday night.

She was committed to a church meeting on Sunday evening but said, "If you don't have other plans, rather than wrestle boxes around your farmhouse tonight, why don't you drop over in an hour or so, and I'll add an extra helping to what I'm cooking and you can join me here? All you have to do is drop by the bakery in town and get a couple of cupcakes for dessert. And maybe you can find at the grocery a bottle of white wine that would work for you."

"That sounds great," said Salt, "but I'm not very dressed up."

"Neither am I," said Margie, "so come as you are."

Salt had time before the bakery and grocery closed to stop by Roy's clothing store. Roy was there—without any help or customers—and looking a bit lonely. "Roy," said Salt, "I need to see your dressiest suits in my size. I may be going to some meetings with some fancy dressers and need to measure up."

"As you can guess," said Roy, "we don't have people who need to dress like that very often, but you're a pretty common size, and we have more in that range than in other sizes. Let's see what I have to add to the navy blue suit you bought last time."

Roy brought down off the rack two chalk-striped suits, one gray and one very dark blue. "These are pretty formal," said Roy. "You'll need some quality white shirts and good ties with these."

Salt wasn't sure what came over him, but he responded, "Fine, let me have both suits, and let's pick out some shirts and ties. And good news, Roy: I don't need the alterations to be done today this time."

"Great," said Roy. "I don't mind telling you that things have been a bit slow, what with the layoffs at the manufacturing plants and the distribution center out on Route 81. I really hope the president gets moving on the trade issues and the virus vaccine and more testing before we all go broke."

"Amen," said Salt.

As Salt walked to his car, he wondered what the hell he was doing. He had just gotten a haircut and bought two suits on the basis that he might be going to some meetings with fancy dressers. He did that without knowing where Stuart's head was—or his own for that matter. And then he agreed to have dinner with Margie without resolving the Louise situation. This did not feel like life simplification.

Salt picked up the necessaries from the bakery and the grocery and, before he forgot and just to further complicate things, called Louise to see if they could have a quiet dinner in the DC area on Sunday evening to give them time to prepare for the Monday-afternoon meeting with Stuart and team that had been confirmed. Louise said Sunday dinner would work.

When Salt arrived at Margie's, she was not dressed to the nines but once again looked very attractive. She was not wearing a black pantsuit. Salt thought to himself that she had been a comfortable and helpful companion at their one dinner and on the few other occasions when they had interacted. That actually meant something.

The discussion over dinner was low-key and unobtrusive. As they finished dinner and the wine, Salt said, "It's good to be back. I just wish the boxes were not waiting for me. My trip was unexpected and got in the way of really moving in."

"Was your trip business or pleasure?" Margie asked.

"Definitely business. I had to go to Europe for a couple of meetings."

"And here I thought you were retired." Margie smiled.

"Fair point," said Salt. But he had to stretch when he continued, "These were sort of follow-on meetings that related to some of what I had done years ago when I was still with the government and then in my law practice. Pretty boring trade stuff."

Margie took that statement as a hint that the subjects of the trip were actually not very boring and that Salt wasn't going to say much more.

"Out of curiosity," Margie asked, "how would you grade President Evans so far?"

"Well," said Salt, "that's a good and fair question. But I think it's too early to tell. There's a lot on the president's plate, and it will likely be a while before we can give the new administration a grade. They have brought in some good people from a pretty broad political spectrum, and that's encouraging."

Salt needed to change the subject, so he asked, "So, how are things with you and Carterville?"

"I'm fine," Margie responded, "but I'm not so sure about Carterville. There have been more layoffs, and the manufacturing slump continues, the downtown stores feel empty, I'm told the real estate market is slow, notwithstanding the low interest rates, and the college is worried about losing even more students over the continuing coronavirus cases and the economy."

"I noticed that Roy's clothing store and the bakery seemed to be pretty empty for a Saturday afternoon," commented Salt.

"You are no doubt right," said Margie, "though a good percentage of the men around here were almost certainly glued to the ACC basketball game this afternoon."

Salt left at 9:45 p.m. after helping with the dishes. There were no awkward moments, though Salt realized that he had finally noticed Margie and recognized her for the very nice person she was. He made a note to himself to be careful. He didn't need more complications.

CHAPTER THIRTY-EIGHT

Rough Seas in DC

The next day, Salt drove to DC for his dinner meeting with Louise at a quiet restaurant in the Tysons area in Northern Virginia, near McLean. During dinner, he explained to Louise the reasons why he did not want to be trapped in the Iran mess. At the core of his reasoning was the fact that Iran could become consuming—and for a long time. Salt was at the point in his life when he wanted to be able to set his own priorities and focus on those. If he wanted to be working on others' priorities, he would have stayed with the law firm.

The Iran situation was tantalizing as a challenge and could achieve much good if successful, but success was a long shot, and it was a foreign relations issue with less domestic impact than others. Salt explained to Louise the inside/outside the Beltway dichotomy that Salt had focused on during his walk in Hyde Park and was driving him. And then there was his desire to do something on the global health front.

Louise listened politely and then took her turn. "That's all well and good for you, Salt, but frankly it's cockeyed and selfish. Where your head is here is all about you. Sure, your new friends in the middle of nowhere in rural Virginia have a role in your thinking, but the reality is that your focus is all about you. That might be understandable and acceptable if you had a snowball's chance of being in the right place at the right time again, but be realistic. So you would like to solve the China trade issues. Great. Just take a number behind Nixon and Kissinger and a hundred others, both dead and alive. The Chinese are wise, patient, and controlling. Some good can come from effective dialogue, but you're not positioned anywhere or with anyone in China. Hell, there are some who think that China is seriously thinking about invading Taiwan. The stakes are too high for someone with your background. Those in front of you with deep ties into the Deep State will wipe you away. Somehow, you have lucked into potentially being in a lead role with the UK and maybe the EU on trade issues, and at the table with Iran. What in God's name makes you think you can replicate that position with trade partners and enemies in Asia? Or do more good? Really?"

Louise had just warmed up. "And then there are others you have conveniently forgotten. Gretchen and I, and to a lesser extent Walter, are willing to put our careers on the line to try to make you look good. Sure, we think we can get something out of it for ourselves, but we can also go down with an aged greenhorn. We have our own balancing act to perform. And your self-centeredness makes a difficult situation much harder."

Salt was taken aback by the vitriol. He had to admit that she had scored a few valid points, but he was nonetheless hurt. And then he blurted out the worst thing that could have passed through his lips: "Is this why you picked the lock to my room in London—to get more control over me?"

She stood up and said, "I can't believe you're enough of a moron to even think that, much less actually say it. Have a good night, Pops." She walked out of the restaurant before the main course was served.

Salt sat alone and picked from both plates but focused more on his cocktail.

Regardless of how good or harmless his intent might have been, he had screwed up big-time. He was sure that Louise was enough of a pro that she would show up at the meeting with Stuart. To not show would be a career-limiting gesture. But she would say very little—at least at first.

Salt decided he would think more about it in the morning but felt that he would most likely just see what Stuart—and Louise—had to say and where the chips would fall. Besides, he had no choice, and there was that nagging grain of truth in what Louise had said. Damn.

CHAPTER THIRTY-NINE

Confession: Good for the Soul and the Mission

This time, the meeting with Stuart was at the State Department. When Salt arrived at Stuart's office at two o'clock on Monday afternoon, he was shown into the very classy waiting room outside Stuart's huge suite of conference rooms and his office. The scene was the real deal. Dark wood, huge rooms, lots of original oil paintings, heavy wood furniture that was mostly antique, and very interesting items from abroad on display. It was a bit like a museum and dripped importance.

Louise was already there in the waiting area. To his surprise, so was Gretchen. Salt had not heard from Louise that morning, and neither Louise nor Gretchen said a word when he arrived. Salt managed only a polite "Good afternoon." This had the makings of an awkward meeting. No, a disastrous meeting.

Stuart called in Salt and Louise but not Gretchen, who may have been there for moral support of Louise.

Salt seized the initiative. "Thanks for making time for us today, Stuart. We appreciate it."

"My pleasure," said Stuart. "We owe you a big debt of gratitude for taking on some interesting situations without much prep time. You should know that we have heard from the Brits and the Germans, and both groups were very complimentary of how you handled yourselves despite being in very tough and unique situations. Both groups are doubtful that we can accomplish much over the long term, but they are fully prepared to undertake reasonable efforts to make what you talked about happen.

"The Germans, of course, are focused on the Iranian situation, which is complex, to say the least. They have not heard back from the Iranians and may not. You were a little curt with them, Salt, but nobody is second-guessing how your team handled things. It seemed pitch perfect. It is possible that we or the Germans will need to call about a follow-up meeting rather than wait for the Iranians to call back. If we ever get beyond first base, the US and German teams would have to be repopulated with more experienced hands, but we would like you to continue there and with the Brits in the short run."

"Thanks for the feedback, Stuart," said Salt. "As you know, neither Louise nor I signed up for these kinds of gigs at the outset. I'm not aware of what Gretchen thinks about all of this. However, if you think we made progress, I'm willing to try to help get both initiatives moving further forward, at least past the launch phase. I have been very impressed with the team you have me working with. Together, we may be short on relevant experience, but Louise and Gretchen are both smart, streetwise, and resourceful. I don't speak for them, and I strongly urge you to talk to them, or at least Louise, separately from me."

"I'm glad to do that, and there's no time like the present," said Stuart.

"There are two other things you need to be aware of, Stuart," said Salt. "First, for a variety of important reasons, if and when it becomes possible, I really would like to have a hand in things related to global health care and Asia. For reasons I would be glad to discuss further with you, this is personal and real. The rationale for the health care interest is obvious, as we discussed when we met with the president. As to Asia, for today, it is enough that I tell you that one of the things our diplomacy needs to display is appreciation of the interests of all Americans, including small businesses. Not all of our trade issues are in the nature of huge global tech matters. Our people need to think we are worried about them as well as our multinationals. There is a connection between foreign affairs and ordinary citizens. I know you know that. We need to preach it more widely so more people recognize the connectivity.

"Second, I sincerely apologize, but while we were in Europe, there were a couple times when Louise and I were under stress and working closely together. Louise is not only very smart but attractive to boot. Nature took its course, and because of my stupidity, things happened. Those things did not, and will not, in my judgment interfere with our working together or separately on this mission. It is not clear to me what will happen with the relationship. Indeed, it may be over. But I need to be straight with you on this: what happened, happened. And, of course, Louise needs to be heard on this."

"Thanks for your candor, Salt," said Stuart, "but what the hell were you thinking?"

Salt knew Stuart did not really expect a response to that, so he stood up, shrugged his shoulders, and headed for the door to leave Stuart's office.

Stuart then opened up on Louise. "Okay—what's your take on both the mission and this messiness?"

Louise sat up and strongly stated, "I'm very interested in staying on this team and working on this initiative. I believe in the mission and think—at least for a while longer—it makes sense to keep the team together. I agree with Salt about the messiness and the uncertainty as to where that's going, and you need to know that everything was consensual and at least as much my fault as Salt's."

"Ugh," muttered Stuart. "Can I assume that there are no embarrassing texts or emails that will show up at a Congressional hearing someday?"

"None," said Louise. "We're smarter than that."

Stuart was clearly not a happy camper but looked up and said, "Okay—you and Salt need to get yourselves down to HR and get this disclosed and papered and do whatever else needs to be done. If we can get this by the HR types, we will continue the team starting later this week. Is Gretchen aware of this, and where is her head?"

"She and I talked at length this morning about everything, and she is on board," said Louise.

"Okay. Catch up with Salt, take him by the ear, and get this straightened out with HR. And send in Gretchen." Stuart looked back down at his desk; the meeting was over.

As Louise was walking out of Stuart's office, she turned around and said to him, "You know, Stuart, it should not be a crime to be human and care for someone, especially if those involved are lonely adults, so long as the caring is not unwelcome."

Stuart looked up and added, "And so long as it does not interfere with the mission."

"Goes without saying," said Louise as she turned back around and finished walking out.

In thirty seconds, Gretchen appeared. Before she could sit down, Stuart asked, "Are you aware of what's been going on, and are you nonetheless interested in staying on the team?"

"Yes, sir," responded Gretchen.

"Okay, good," said Stuart. "Were you involved in anything inappropriate on this mission?"

"No, sir," responded Gretchen.

Stuart sighed and said, "Very good, and thank you. Now get going and make sure the other two don't screw this up. They may need a witness down in HR."

Stuart thought for a few minutes and then called in his assistant and asked him to set up a meeting with Salt, Louise, Gretchen, and Walter in two days, and to get the Iran situation on the president's agenda as soon as possible.

Stuart silently hoped that some of the inherited crises and dysfunction would soon abate. That would be a good thing. But until then, there was a mountain of issues to attend to. And he needed good help, even if they came with a few warts.